DIRT

A CELESTIA FANTASY ADVENTURE

MICHELLE HASKEW

For Mike, who changed my entire world, pulled me from the bottomless pit and helped me discover the strength to fulfil my dreams. My love is an ocean, a story without end.
Adore you forever Husband.

DIRT

"Essentially, all life depends on the dirt...There can be no life without dirt and no dirt without life; they have evolved together."
Charles Edwin Kellogg

DIRTY SECRETS

DIRTY PASTS

DIRTY LIES

ONLY WHEN YOU ARE TRULY ALONE, WHEN LIFE HAS GROUND YOU INTO THE DIRT, WHEN YOU ARE SCATTERED, CAN YOU ALTER. OVER TIME YOU REFORM, YOU BECOME DENSER, STRONGER, HARDENED.
WHAT EMERGES FROM THE DIRT IS THE CAPTIVATING   CREATION THAT YOU WERE ALWAYS MEANT TO BE.

CHAPTER 1

BLUE

Blue trudged across the muddy field, exhausted. Her muscles screamed and her brain seemed like it was filled with dirt. Clayish, tough, brick-like dirt that refused to yield to her spade. Stubborn dirt, that made her thoughts grimy. Her jarring steps, tentative and slow, caused her neck and back to flare with a tormented burning.

As she navigated across the boggy ground, towards her treehouse, she looked up into the swirling skies. She breathed in the fresh air, feeling grateful for the mildness of the day. Some days, Celestia was an oven.

Cloaked in clouds, the faint sun's heat upon her skin was a gentle, pleasant caress. It was not like the last few days in The Elysium Meadows. The land where they toiled was a completely different story. Back in the Elysium Meadows, the noxious pollution made each breath feel like inhaling grit. The intense humidity often zapped her energy. Like a lid, the clouds trapped in the muggy, choking air; it simmered whilst Blue and the other workers roasted. Coupled with the back-breaking forage for food, it often made each moment seem like an hour. Still, it was vital. They had to eat. They had quotas to meet. Recently, Blue was frustrated by the pace, the pressure had risen; Calete Company were supplying the Capital Core now.

It was an important deal for the Caletes, that meant a growing burden on Blue and the rest of the foragers.

Shaded by tall trees, the cleaner air of Hallowed Brook was a relief from the foraging fields. The gilded rays of sun were desperately trying to tear through the moody clouds. Here and there a finger of light had found purchase and stubbornly raked at the grey. Blue turned her face up to the golden shards and relished the feel of the pleasant heat upon her chilled skin. She stopped to stand in the mud, breathing in the fresher air and soaking up the warmth. It had been unusually chilly in the meadow today, damp too. These unexpected lower temperatures made her spinal pain much more pronounced. She stretched, wincing at the unnatural clicking of her bones. Her face mask, hanging down from her chin, was coated in a solid layer of grime.

As the slit in the sky became a larger, gaping hole, Blue stood a little longer, bathing in the rays of the shimmering sun. She looked like an ethereal being, angelic, for a fleeting second at least. Suddenly, she was drowned in a dense black shadow, her time in the healing warmth broken. Far above her, a Devout Drolle, the huge creature with a magnificent wingspan, flew high. Effortlessly it swooped and soared. It's agile flight and gentle trilling caws, took her mind up into the vast heavens. Up into the infinite blue.

Mesmerised, she watched the creature's sapphire and amber feathers ruffle in the swirling breeze. The bird's head, and its golden beak, were steadfastly trained towards the threads of tinted clouds that lined the horizon. It would be seeking out prey: small birds, and mammals, to take back to its mate and chicks upon the upper reaches of the Desire Mountains. The wild bird was enormous, a true thing of beauty.

Blue stood transfixed. Her shoulders relaxed slightly as she watched. In seconds, her taut muscles seemed to ease. As she tracked the bird's magnetic movements, her mind slowly began to still too. It held a hypnotic, meditative power as it dived and rolled, gliding in the heavens above their village. Within minutes, the soaring creature had disappeared, arcing off beyond the horizon. Its retreating flight was graceful and free.

Rumour had it that these colossal, feathered beasts had once been trained in order to be flown by the ancestors. The many, heavily embellished stories recounted that they had been ridden by the Celestians of the past. As she thought of the awe that the bird made rise within her, Blue was certain that this was a myth from some elders' overactive imagination. It couldn't have happened, surely. To Blue, the Devout Drolle looked far too wild to have ever been even partially constrained. It was a beast with sharp talons and a sharp mind of its own. To fly it would have required considerable taming of that energy.

Turning from the skies, Blue focused her aquamarine eyes back on the area she called home. Under the treetop houses, the muddy land was still. Rain earlier had made the dirt a boggy quagmire, she knew that ice had melted in the high up mountains too. She watched as it trickled down in thin rivulets, adding to the deluge, but the sun was now casting a wide, warm light; the afternoon clouds had been temporarily parted. Perhaps the ground might even harden a little this evening. That would be a rarity.

Hallowed Brook was quiet this early in the day, most of its inhabitants were still completing their work duties. Blue had managed to sneak off early. Well, she'd been ordered to leave her post really. This was one of the perks of being close friends with Troy, the overseer at Elysium Meadow.

Friends...

Troy had seen the pain that was stark in her eyes, the way that Blue had desperately tried not to grimace with each and every downward stroke of her spade. He knew that her smile was forced, that her eyes, trained to the ground, hid her agony. Troy knew her too well. He effortlessly read each imperceptible movement. He knew her in the dark. Troy had dug himself into her mind, mired within her consciousness and, try as she might, she couldn't dislodge him.

Did she want to dislodge him?

Blue shivered. Thoughts of Troy had momentarily unbalanced her, and a pleasant warmth radiated within. A flare of desire ached, and she gasped, the flash of its intensity making her disorientated. She blushed with a sense of surprise. Despite her tense neck, taut back, the throb in her spine, she imagined his brown hands, rough from work, tangling in her hair, his soft lips pressing against hers as his tongue dipped to taste her own. Heart pounding, her fickle body betrayed her. She sighed, confused. She wasn't completely sure about him.

Get a grip Blue, get a grip, and get some sleep.

The familiar voice that echoed around her heavy head, was that of her dearest friend. Her only true friend really, Jess.

Jess and Blue had often known exactly what the other was thinking, without words. The pair had been connected intuitively, for as long as Blue could remember. Since early childhood. It was as if they'd trodden the path of life hand in hand, meandering through the curves, knowing they would always have someone to rely on. No longer though. Jess had vanished. She had disappeared, gone like a whisper on the breeze. With her she had taken fragments of Blue's fragile heart.

When it had happened, part of Blue's world had ground to a screeching stop. She had been turned to mush, like the very ground they worked. When Jessie didn't return, when the days turned into weeks, into months, then she'd struggled to find some solidity. She'd forced herself to stand tall again, to get on with things as well as she could. But, in her heart she knew she had been forever changed by the loss. Blue often sagged under the weight of her reality.

She missed her best friend with a sharp, stabbing, slice to the heart. Sliced and torn, this was a hurt like no other. Yes, Jess had taken a chunk of Blue's heart with her when she left. The gap that remained ached; a throbbing hole that seemed as if it could never, ever be filled. The edges were raw, shredded, tender and the very mention of Jess, thoughts of her, ripped at the wound anew. Even when it was just the memory of her upbeat, teasing words, words rhythmically echoing around her head. The way they always did. To Blue, it seemed as if barely a moment went by without her skittish brain fixating on thoughts of Jess and, often, she spent hours wracking her memories, trying to summon up some snippet that might give her answers. Her grey matter was always working, wondering where the hell she could be, or if she was even still alive.

Please let her be alive.

She breathed out a heavy breath, glancing over at Jessie's treehouse. Blue didn't want to consider the fact that she may be dead. She sighed again heavily; she was still adrift without her. She hated to face up to it, but it was true. Some days she was pretty sure she was drowning. Flailing around without a chance.

Where are you, Jess? Why haven't you come home yet?

After the initial paralysis, Jessie's disappearance had plunged Blue into a thick, cloying pit of despair. She'd never been so low. It was a murky pit, lacking light, with a long, slow upward climb that gave scant chance of escape. The pit had sticky; claylike walls that made Blue continually slide back down. Plunging, whenever she made the slightest progress upwards. Each time she thought she had reached a glimpse of the sunshine; something reminded her of what she had lost, and her unsteady grip on the slippery, crumbling handholds had faltered. She tumbled back into the gloom. Her tenacity gone.

Was Jessie gone forever too?

Blue shook her head. She shook away the oppressive thoughts like she was clearing away gravel. This wallowing wouldn't help, it just widened the weeping wound, causing her to be pushed back into the pit. It had been three months now. Three long months of pure torture. She hadn't slept properly for weeks, and Jessie haunted her dreams. Dread hung like a constant shadow, menacingly dark, at the periphery of her vision. Like an ever present, dense bleakness threatening to overpower her. She needed to rest. Blue stumbled slightly, feeling tiredness wash over her, forcing her to focus on keeping her eyes open. To watch her step.

Her treehouse was only a short distance away, and she carefully inched her way across the divots and clods of gloopy black soil. Sometimes, before Jess had gone on days where her spine wasn't radiating with sharp tenderness, she would splash in the silty puddles chuckling, Jess giggling and holding her sides, but not today. She tried to avoid jolting her throbbing back which seemed more and more aggravated with each painful step.

At the bottom of the treehouse ladder, Blue shook off her work boots, carefully placing them in her boot store. Bending to do so made her lower back screech shrilly in complaint. Then, barefoot, she gingerly climbed the wooden rungs up to her small sanctuary.

Blue's head was spattered with a thousand dark thoughts, saturated in pools of gloom. She carelessly stripped off her filth smeared overalls as she walked towards her bed, dropping each sodden garment like she was shedding responsibilities. Casting the clothes aside like her worries; discarding the cloying layers that weighed her down. With a piercing meow, Scruffy, her cat fled.

"Hey, sorry Scruffs."

Blue knew she should wash. She smelt of hard work, pain, and anxious worry. The grimy sweat had settled on her skin like a frigid blanket. She was slick with the scum of hours of digging.

Naked, she fell without grace, into a heap on the

circular, already rumpled bed. Getting clean would wait. She had been worse, this wasn't disgustingly vile, and besides the bed was already in need of changing.

The creased, multicoloured covers smelt of him. The scent enveloped her as, despite her nagging back, she began to drift into a heavy, deep sleep.

Jess, please, tell me, where are you?

This swirling question muddied her last thoughts and brought with it, sludgy, dense dreams.

***

It was dark by the time Blue surfaced; the skies beyond her window were sprinkled with a thousand stars. She felt a heavy arm encircle her waist and the heat of another body pressed languidly against her.

Troy.

He lay by her side naked, his arm lazily thrown across her core. She envied how relaxed he seemed to be in that moment. Sometimes, in the fields, he carried his responsibility like a weighty boulder. He often brooded with hooded eyes and a faraway gaze.

The bright crocheted blankets had been shed like snakeskin. It was a warm, pleasant night and, in the silvery moonlight, Troy looked like a sculptured marble statue. The skilled work of a truly brilliant artist. His smooth, brown skin seemed sheened in alabaster.

Part of her was angry, irritated by Troy, by his ease, by his presence. It felt intrusive, just joining her on her bed in the night. It niggled away at the pit of her stomach, it felt lacking in consent. Did his privilege mean he thought he could act however he liked? That he could do as he pleased because he was a Calete? But another part of Blue welcomed the soothing sensation of bare skin against bare skin. His skin. The familiar sound of Troy's steady breathing, and the undeniable way that he made her feel secure.

Does he make you feel secure though?

Not wanting to wake him, knowing he'd had a really tough week down in the fields, she slid carefully from under his inert, muscular arm and tiptoed out of the treehouse doors, out onto her veranda, into the warm night.

With the clouds now gone, the planet was hosting an underrated light show. A billion balls of fiery gas lit up the obsidian sky. Pinpricks glowing from many other galaxies, other solar systems, other far-off places. The moon was a perfect disk, its stolen light making the Brook glow. The illumination spellbinding.

Blue raised her clenched neck, took a deep breath, and watched the twinkling in the stillness above her. It was magical. The sky looked almost as if it had been painted on canvas. Like one of Jessie's paintings. An idyllic, dreamlike representation of the heavenly realm. She focused on one bright star, one that seemed to flutter like a firefly.

Was someone up on one of those tiny specks of light, staring out into the dark like she was?

Blue's mind automatically hovered and settled. Like always, it settled on thoughts of Jessie. Her Jessie. Like beating wings, her heart fluttered.

Where could she be?

Could Jess see this same sky? Or was she gone…gone

forever...lost?

She slipped into the past then, easily drifting into her childhood days with Jessie.

They were always two peas in a pod really. Destined to be in each other's lives. Their path alongside one another seemed written in the very stars, the ones she was standing here gazing up at.

The bonds they had formed as children had only strengthened when they had come of age. Two curvy brunettes, never quite fitting into their clothes, in-tune with each other. Each of them had blue eyes, although Jessie's weren't quite as shockingly intense as Blue's were. Blue had piercing ocean eyes, hence the name she had been given.

People always commented that they were both feisty, full of fun, free spirits. She loved that Jessie was a force to be reckoned with, a whirlwind of energy, always up for an adventure. Her charisma was contagious, she was always wanting to explore, to do something new. Jess was spontaneous, obsessed with snatching every single speck of joy out of the day, embracing all that she possibly could. She thrived on exploring. Perhaps that was why she was gone. Was she off up a mountain tracking down some rare mammal? Was she making notes in her journal? Drawing doodles and penning small snippets of poetry?

No. Blue knew that she wouldn't have left for so long without finding some way to get a message back to her, she would have tried anyway at all. They were each other's family. After what had happened with their parents, the pox. Despite them having gone through so much pain together, they had taken solace in their bond.

Jessie had always been far more fearless than her. Her friend laughed in the face of danger and saw peril as a prey to be hunted down and wrestled into submission. Her friend thrived on pushing herself to the very limit. Perhaps, she had pushed herself too far. There were dangerous creatures everywhere on Celestia. Their environment, especially beyond the settlements, could be perilously hostile.

Would she ever come back?

A familiar melancholy cloaked Blue, it was like a scratchy old sweater. As her eyes searched the overwhelming darkness for answers, she felt the unsettling irritation. When she dropped her gaze from the light show in the heavens, Hallowed Brook was pitch black. No lights in the canopy, no lights on the ground. It took Blue's eyes some time to adjust. Dots of glittery white swirled like ghosts behind her lids.

They were required to save resources. It was the latest commands. The nightly shutdown was Central Core dictated. A direct order from Longford Grimes, their President. Whispers and gossip had it that the planet's fossil fuel supplies were becoming dangerously depleted. They were rumoured to be at emergency levels, crisis point. Blue wasn't sure what to think.

This 'Central Regime Energy Drive' plunged the whole Brook area into pitch black nothingness. Some found it oppressive, they questioned the rationale. It had caused controversy and wild, rambling whispers of conspiracies. Some of the villagers said it was a sign, that there was something the Capital Core was hiding. Others argued it was because of dark magic.

Who knew... was something sinister afoot?

Blue found the solid blackness kind of comforting. Especially now. She wanted her whole mind to be as empty as the atmosphere here in Hallowed Brook. The opaque nothingness that swallowed the village after dark. She desperately wanted to be free from any flashes of painful memories, from the loneliness of her loss; cocooned in the gentle glow of candlelight.

Despite it being well before dawn, a warm breeze caressed her skin and for a brief moment she felt utterly free. As free as she had been back before it had happened. Back in those crazy times when she had spent hours doubled up with laughter, relaxed beside Jess. Free like the Saint Blurt, the four-legged whirlwind of an animal, with a white coat and a bright scarlet free-flowing mane, that hurtled across their planet without a care in the world. The Saint Blurt had always been Jessie's spirit animal.

She tried to pinch that unique feeling between her fingers, like she had to pinch the writhing worms out in the fields. She wanted to hold onto it, to never ever let it go.

She heard a faint stirring behind her, and her stomach momentarily sank. The breath caught fast in her throat. Blue had no energy for emotions right now, no patience for discussion. She didn't want to think. She just wanted to be lost in the black, blind to everything, with a guarantee that, by morning, there would be new light.

***

He was behind her.

"Hey Blue, why are you up? Come back to bed. It's too early. You need rest," whispered Troy. His hair was gently tousled, his body partially lit by the small flickering candles that he must have used to find his way across the sodden fields. He'd put them on the floor by her treehouse doorway, carefully placing them in her wooden lanterns. Troy's voice was deep with the sedative effects of sleep. Her eyes lingered briefly on his chest. The shards of moonlight made him look as if he were a divine being.

She turned away.

Blue bristled with irritation. How dare he tell her what to do. Did he think she was some little woman who needed his guidance, who needed a man to look out for her? Did he think she was stupid?

Fire flared in her chest; she was angry that he'd just turned up without saying he would. He wasn't her boss here. This wasn't his foraging field where he could tell her what to do.

Her mind fluttered about like the butterflies that danced around the rock face behind the forest. Part of her adored his company, part of her liked being alone. Alone was safer. Alone meant less hurt. And there was Jessie's warning lingering like a bad stench.

"I'm fine Troy, honestly. What made you come over here? I wasn't expecting you," She heard the ice tinkling in her voice. She couldn't seem to keep it out.

"Blue, c'mon, you know why. I knew you were struggling, that's why I let you go early. From the fields. I wanted to check in on you. You were dead to the world Blue, so peaceful. The look on your face was... I just climbed in alongside you. I'm sorry. Do you...um... mind?" His voice caught on the last sentence, and she realised she was being unfair...spiky. He cared. He was her friend.

Blue was just so used to being alone. Well, alone apart from Jessie. They tended to fend for themselves. Dancing to their own tune. Life had always been step by step, a glorious adventure alongside Jessie. Even their dark days had been side by side.

"Troy, honestly, it's fine. I'm fine. I'm tired still. In pain. I ache. You know how it's been. My neck...my back... it grinds me down...you know, it takes over. It's getting worse. And...well, I woke up thinking about Jess. I couldn't get her face out of my head." Blue's eyes dipped down to the wooden deck of the treehouse. She tried to block out the stiffness, the soreness that pierced her. An oppressive silence followed. It wove around them like fog.

A short creak of the treehouse's ancient boards told Blue that he was coming to hold her. She stubbornly stepped back, moving further from his arms.

"Blue... hey, c'mon... don't..."

She turned and raised her eyes to his defiantly. Something flashed in her, like she'd been scraped by her spade. It stung.

"I'm good Troy. Honest. You don't need to be here. I can take care of myself. I always have. Always. I don't need you. I don't want you to think that I need you..."

As the words left her mouth, she tasted the bitterness that they were laced in. The sharp poison stung her tongue.

He reeled back suddenly, as if slapped.

"Troy, I..."

It was too late. The words had begun to work their way around his veins. Their effect was almost immediate, he was shutting down. She saw it clearly in his eyes.

It didn't take long for those poisoned words to stop up his heart. It was like watching someone, vibrantly alive, suddenly turn to stone. Like the effects of an evil spell, a sorceresses' magic. He hardened.

As she flushed with a brief stab of shame, his face became a stony mask. His lips set into a grim line.

"You're right. I get it. I'll go, I'll go now, Blue," Troy whispered turning his back on her. He stood bare and vulnerable, in the amber glow of the candles. As she wrestled with her tangled feelings, Troy moved inside slowly to dress.

For a while, the silence felt palpable. It was dank, heavy, and underneath the quiet, it was teeming with the hidden creatures that scurry unseen in the night; the ugly things that lie buried.

Blue somehow found her voice, following him inside. The small, circular house was cramped with tension.

"Yes. I think it's for the best Troy," Blue replied trying to blunt the force of each syllable. She shut her eyes as he stood with his back still turned to her. She was momentarily embarrassed by her obvious desire to hurt him. It wasn't the desire he was used to.

A memory of Jess formed crystal clear. Vivid and sharp, the recollection swirled behind her eyelids. It unsteadied her, and she concentrated hard to stay balanced. Jess had been uncharacteristically sombre that day, her blue eyes had appeared haunted, her head down, her posture tense. She had looked around cautiously, filled with a nervous jitteriness before she spoke.

"Be careful Blue. I just want to protect you. Please be careful. You know the history, who he is, where he comes from. That family. The Caletes…Is it really a good idea to get mired in all of that?" The words were whispered as if saying them too loudly could be dangerous.

Her friend had looked cowed. Her carefree devil-may-care attitude shredded. Blue watched as Jess had nibbled at her fingers, her eyes blinking. Something deeper had been bugging her. Why was she intensely trying to warn Blue about Troy that day?

Jessie, please come back.

"I know you miss her…" Troy turned. His eyes were numb though, emotionless. His protective barriers firmly raised. Troy's mouth was fixed into a tense grimace as he had shrugged on his jeans and t-shirt. He folded his arms, protecting his heart.

Of course, he knew. He knew Blue like the very land they worked together. He knew her like he knew how to breathe: Unconsciously, intuitively, instinctively.

"I do," Blue replied flatly.

"There's still a chance that she'll return Blue. There is. She'll walk into the Brook one day with her tales of the far reaches of the planet, triumphant. I tell you, she'll come back with fire in her eyes and a swagger in her step. She'll come to me demanding her job back and then quit again after a few weeks. She's not gone forever, I'm sure. Keep hoping hey? She can't be gone for good Blue. It may happen. We all want her home."

Some warmth had returned to his words. It was Troy, try as he might, he could never stay mad for long. His face looked flushed; he was willing the utterances to be true.

Troy's words misted the air. The breath vanished, mixing with the darkness, unseen. His words were gone in an instant; insubstantial words that had become an invisible part of the atmosphere. Gone like Jess. Gone without a trace. Gone without retrieval. Try as she might, Blue couldn't bring them back. They had slipped upon the early morning air, found a drift, meandering to a place where they could no longer be captured, forever out of reach.

"It's been almost three months Troy. This isn't normal. Her regular treks were mere days, not weeks and certainly not months. This is different. It feels different. I just know."

Something indistinct seemed to flash in Troy's eyes then, something Blue couldn't read. He looked troubled somehow, worried. He looked to the floor and bit his lip. A wistfulness wavered in his gaze, as he became buried in her words. Blue replayed their conversation over, she knew had hurt him. It was becoming a habit. She softened slightly, feeling ashamed, deeply regretting her earlier gall.

"Look, Troy, I need more sleep, lots more. I could literally sleep for a week. Stay. Don't head back. Stay with me. It's too late to trek back out across the mud. You'll fall. Break something. Can't have two of us in agony. Let's go back to bed boss. To rest. Just rest. And, just so you know, I'm calling in sick tomorrow. Your quotas can go to hell!"

Troy grinned despite himself, and the tension left his body. He blew out a half laugh, half breath. The dimples in his cheeks turned her to mush.

She felt his choked exhale flow out through his flesh, out onto the veranda, out into the canopy, out into the night. A wisp of pain caused by her rash words that danced in the darkness, the wisp somersaulted on the breeze, it diluted as it rose ever upwards towards the stars. The bitterness was gone, mixed with the intangible words he'd whispered before, the words of Jessie's return.

"Stuff my quotas? Well, you know Blue if that's the case, I'll have to cut your rations. I'm the boss. I make the decisions. Call in sick? How very dare you, underling, the damned impertinence," Troy laughed again, the noise like melodic bells, his voice teasing and playful. The sound made her feel lighter.

"Go ahead. Cut 'em Boss. See if I care," Blue chuckled quietly, "Seems I'll just have to eat you instead."

White hot electricity crackled between them.

Blue moved towards Troy with a raw hunger. She wanted to feel the weight of him upon her. She wanted the touch of his fingers, the heat of his limbs and the delicious way that he knew exactly what made her arch her back, scream his name. He made her lose her mind. She wanted Troy to engulf her. To bury her like a landslide.

She took his hand and led him back to the tangled blankets on the circular bed. Helping him shed his clothes in a choreographed dance with which they were familiar. The heat of her mouth was already upon his lips, his neck. Her fatigue had vanished, the insistent pain forgotten.

Neither of them were paying much attention to the darkness, neither of them noticed the watching eyes, neither of them realised that they were being observed.

Hidden within the canopy, concealed in the dense foliage, a red laser mechanically pulsed back and forth. The conversation had been recorded, the information transmitted, the relevant authorities were notified.

Gathering dirt.

CHAPTER 2

TROY

It was like she was a magnet. He couldn't help being drawn to her. Attracted by some hypnotic pull. Try as he might, every time he tore his eyes away, he couldn't stop them from seeking her out again. His gaze settling on her familiar form. It drove him mad.

It was cooler today. Dry at least, but cooler. There was a pervasive dampness hanging in the thick air and the sky had a steely, metallic tinge, it reflected the grey mood that seemed to have buried him. His chest was tight from the grimy air and the reality he didn't want to face head on.

Blue didn't realise the profound effect that she had on him. Drawn back to her once more, he watched her work, spotting that the discomfort, as she dug, was disguised by a wry, fixed smile. He knew though. He knew that she was hiding the pain, forcing it down, carrying on. He could see that Blue was digging deep into her endless reserves of grit and determination.

She was so strong.

She had noticed him watching, her head rising momentarily before returning to the ground. Blue, had moved to a deeper part of the field where he couldn't see her as clearly, tucking herself away from his gaze. He knew she was uncomfortable with the scrutiny, she never wanted special treatment, or, for others to know about them. She valued her privacy and hated to think that they were the talk of the fields. Ky knew, and Jess had known but she kept her cards very close to her chest, the king and queens of her hand hidden.

Still, he moved himself so he could still see her. She worked so hard, diligently digging and sifting through the dirt. Her bucket always brimmed with root vegetables: enough to feed twenty or more. Separately she had kept a tub of insects and worms: Protein. Most people's buckets were near empty, the graft was painstaking. But, Troy knew that she was using the back-breaking toil as a distraction. He knew that she was burying a mountain of grief.

His heart felt bolstered, merely glimpsing Blue's steadily moving form drove him insane, centring him at the same time. She gave him balance as well as knocking him off his feet. If only she felt the same.

A blur quickly crossed his vision as a mucky, ham-like hand was waved in front of his face. A hand thick with smeared dirt. "Control to Troy, come in Troy, return to Celestia we're losing you, buddy...ahh... too late... he's gone," teased the familiar voice of his best friend, Ky.

Troy returned Ky's playful poking with a steely glare of his chestnut eyes. He held his tongue.

"Man, you have it bad. The look on your dumb face Boss. It's priceless. Just priceless! Troy and Blue sitting in a tree K I S S I N G."

"Quit it Ky. Quit it now. People are listening, they always are, always," he hissed the words through gritted teeth. He heard the iron threaded within his response, soldered into each syllable.

Troy knew that Ky was merely poking fun, having a laugh at his expense but, there was a danger in his attraction to Blue. He was supposed to maintain a level of hierarchy over his workforce. He had the respectability of his family name to uphold too. The ever-present, heavy burden of his ancestry. The Calete reputation…he thought with a wry smile. And, he knew for a fact Eliza wouldn't approve.

"Chill out Troy, no one is interested in what we say, the powers that be don't give a damn about us minions. I promise you that!" Ky laughed and his amber eyes scrunched at the edges.

But he wasn't just a minion, was he? Not at all.

The high-pitched giggle that burst from his friends lips was at odds with his massive frame. Ky was a hulk of a man with a solidity that often intimidated. His friend was known as a heartbreaker. A man who worked hard and played hard. Troy had seen Ky sifting through the coarse mud with the same determination that he sifted through the eligible females on Celestia. He always managed to find his fill of food to sign off on his buckets, as well as a steady stream of female friends. The gods had smiled on Ky, blessing him with charm, wit, a caustic sense of humour and endless energy. He was full of spirit, light in his words and with a lightness of heart.

Occasionally he could be a total idiot, but he was Troy's best friend.

His slightly squeaky voice belied his assured

masculinity. He'd been hit on by thirsty men more times than Troy could count. Ky always took it in good humour, but he was clear that he definitely preferred the company of women.

"I'm sending her back to her treehouse," Troy mused aloud. The words left his mouth before he realised that this snippet of information wasn't really Ky's to have.

"Hey Boss, you're in charge, I'm merely the hired muscle. You, my friend, can deal with your workers however you feel," he winked. "In the meantime, I'll be over there, foraging. Someone has got to keep their mind on finding food, right?"

"Ky, I mean it," Troy hissed.

Ky left with another wink, his blonde hair catching the light like a damned halo. Troy spotted the distinct bounce in his step. For some reason he thrived out here in the fields. Whilst most of the workers despised the gloopy mud, the persistent rain, the humidity, and pollution, for his friend Ky, it was like a sport. He treated each new day as a competition, a quest. Blue and Ky were Troy's best workers as well as being his friends.

Troy thought of different ways to tell Blue to leave her post. To send her home. He knew that it wouldn't be easy, that she'd resist like tough, stony ground. He moved sentences around in his head like he was sifting through soil. Turning the right words over and then digging in for more when they didn't seem to settle right. He needed it perfect. Damn, this was hard. He'd never felt like this before, like each word mattered. Each single utterance had weight. The way it fell made a difference. He realised that Blue was the difference.

In the end, he steeled himself and headed across the clawing mud to her. He'd just tell her. He needed to stop overthinking. He was the boss after all.

Shoulders hunched; he approached Blue with an apprehensive wave.

***

When she was gone, even though there were only a few hours left until clock off, he felt her absence like a sink hole.

It had begun to get warmer, the sun peeking through the murky clouds, and sweat trickled from his furrowed brow as he counted the minutes until shutdown. Troy and the remaining workers sweltered.

He decided he would go and see her later. She might not welcome his presence, but he ached for her.

He had fallen for her a long time ago. Almost as soon as he had met her. It stung a little that she was still largely indifferent to him. At least they had their time together though.

Suddenly, a huge Devout Drolle cast a large shadow over the meadow. Many workers stopped and looked up into the grey, smoggy skies. Some of them removed their grimy facemasks so that they could get a better view of the streamlined bird.

Troy craned his neck and felt his chest swell with the magnificence of the sight.

Despite them being native to the meadows, a regular visitor from the icy mountain slopes, these elegant beasts had a presence that inspired fascination. He had been told, years back, when he was a boy, that his great grandfather could fly these majestic creatures. Erodan, his father's, father's father had apparently used the agility of the Devout Drolles to build some of the higher up treehouses. The large birds had made it easier for the ancestors to access the treehouse roofs. To thatch the larger structures.

Troy had been told many stories. His ancestors had been integral to creating the co-existent community here. The Caletes were founders of this part of the planet: The farming and food production lands. They ran the fields, built the houses, made the rules, decided who did what.

It was one of the reasons that he had been given a leadership role at such a young age. He was barely twenty-five and had been in his post for the last two years. As always, family names often opened doorways that were firmly shut to most. He recognised the power of his name. It embarrassed him. Troy knew full well that the Calete's pasts were connected to secrets and lies.

Some days, he wished he could relinquish this responsibility and just be free. Free like the mammoth bird they were watching right at this moment. He felt the weight of his role like large clods of hard to break mud. Sometimes he was sure that he was drowning, sinking down, choking. The very soil they worked threatening to suffocate him.

The Devout Drolle soared high into the peaks of the mountains. Its elegant wingspan taking it out of view. Troy sighed, running his fingers through his black mop of hair, fixing his face mask before he returned to the task of supervising his team of foragers. They had quotas to meet after all. Ky was right, people had to eat, and he had to keep production going. There was greater pressure now;

supplies around the planet were dwindling.

He would definitely check in on Blue later though. Whether she liked it or not.

***

He lay nestled with Blue, their earlier fight forgotten, instead they intwined, warm and glowing. Sometimes he felt as if their minds were at complete odds with each other, enemies. But their bodies, well it couldn't be denied that their bodies were friends.

She awoke something in him that no one else ever had. The feeling was hypnotic, it made him forget the weight of his responsibility, just for a short while.

As she slept upon his chest, her long brown hair creating a wave across his skin, he thought back to what she had said earlier out on the veranda. Her words had been hard to swallow. They had choked him. He could still sense the remnants of the bile behind them; it stung his lips. But, he understood, he knew she had a lot to deal with at the moment. Troy was aware of how she was consumed with worry for Jess. He'd seen how she'd behaved out of character, acting irrationally.

Hell, if she heard him say that he'd be dead meat.

A memory stirred.

Troy's heart began to pound, and his stomach was filled with fluttering black moths, ones that sought out shadows within the cover of darkness. Death Head moths, their huge wingspan an omen. He gulped, hoping not to wake Blue. She couldn't see what was in his chestnut eyes right now; not now and not ever.

Troy's body froze as his eyes glistened with unshed tears of guilt. Guilt, regret, and inaction. He was paralysed with the weight of what he knew, keeping in the hurt.

The woman he loved lay sleeping here in his arms, and he had done nothing about the intense pain that tortured her every day.

Troy had done nothing. Nothing about Jess. Nothing about the knowledge he had discovered. He tried not to think about the reason why Jess had been taken. But, his thoughts kept returning to the theory, his theory, like he was worrying a fresh scab.

He couldn't do anything. His hands were bound. If he revealed what he knew, then it could threaten them all.

Troy knew he was a coward. The dilemma was eating him up daily. If he didn't talk to someone soon it would completely consume him.

Troy made a decision then and there. He allowed his shoulders to relax as the determination took away some of his built-up tension. He closed his weary eyes, feeling the ebony, portentous moths calming inside him. They now merely flickered, settling and resting within. At least that was something.

He would go up into the mountains tomorrow and get some much-needed guidance. Troy had decided to seek out The Visionary.

CHAPTER 3

JESS

Drip. Drip. Drip. Endless drips were the soundtrack to her life now. The regular, repetitive thuds almost drove her insane. How she had managed to hold it together for so long was a mere miracle.

Cold and damp iced the air of the bitterly frigid, shadowy cave. Beneath her loosely bound body, the rough, jagged stone jabbed into her continually. Jess felt fragile, like her bones were made of fine porcelain: delicate and breakable.

She tried to stretch any muscles that she could move. Each day she knew she was seizing up more and more, until eventually she would cease to be a person, instead she would become part of the stony ground, like a fossil.

Jess weakly moved her limbs. She hated the pervasive feeling of weakness more than anything else. With a sigh, she pushed down her despondency, otherwise it would overwhelm her. She could take pain, she could take the constant surveillance, the harsh words, but, feeling weak, that pushed her under, into the depths.

Jess had always been robust and strong, mentally strong and physically strong. Three months of this hell had reduced her to a brittle, vulnerable shell. She despised what they had done. She knew that lately, every noise, every scratch, every scrape, every shuffle jangled her nerves. As she lay on the unforgiving, chilled floor, she made a vow, she would ensure that those who had done this to her paid.

Three months was a long time to lie alone with your thoughts. It was a long time to endure the terrible food, the swampy, green water, the tethers. Most of all though, it was a long time to be without her best friend. She had scratched the sunsets and sunrises, tallies upon the softer stone, a record of her capture. A record of how long she had been away from Blue.

Her eyes were heavy, her head foggy, as she thought about the last time she had seen her, and what she wished she had said to her.

Jess usually talked to Blue every day. In fact, even though the conversation was one way here, she continued to talk to her friend multiple times a day. It was just in her head though. All in her head. A ramble, a one-sided babble.

Jessie's inner dialogue had kept her sane. If she hadn't had the regular back and forth conversations with Blue in her mind, she knew she might have tried to end it all. She could have found a way. Sometimes the despair eclipsed her desire to keep breathing. Her blue eyes stared blank-eyed at the shallow puddles; she knew that they could be a way out if she was brave enough.

Yes, Jessie acknowledged the truth, talking to Blue within her head had kept her alive.

The darkness and near silence made Jessie's senses nerve wrackingly acute. She heard the calls of birds, the sounds of the animals, as if they were in the cave with her.

The gentle caw of the mighty Devout Drolle, occasionally the echoing roar of Pilgrim Cats, and the hooves of Saint Blurts as they cantered wildly across the plains. She recognised the whinnies of the sleek beasts, the rhythmic swish of their tails. She could picture their pure snowy coats, their scarlet manes. Perhaps if she could find a way out, if she could entice one, she could ride it home.

Hey, it's not some damned fairy tale girl.

The imagined words made her smile for a brief second. Jess suspected that she was hidden within the mountains somewhere. A range of mountains. There were many on Celestia. Mountains were like the bones of the planet, sticking out all across its surface. Bones of starvation, bones of want.

When she listened closely, Jessie often heard the raging of fast flowing water, like waterfalls cascading. And the sound of the rain was a constant. Yes, she was pretty sure that she was in a cave system within one of the planets mountain ranges. Maybe, she hoped, she wasn't that far from where they had taken her. Then, she would know her way home. Behind her home, in Hallowed Brook, the Desire Mountains painted the sky. Their peaks causing heavy rainfall. The clouds' tears filled the lakes and rivers. She had started to make a mental map of this place in her mind.

Sometimes, for hours at a time, she would think *why me?* Ultimately though, Jess knew that this was futile. There was probably zero rhyme or reason to why she had been taken. It was likely just an accident rather than by design. Like the way that predators chose their prey. The truth was that sometimes it was simply a case of the wrong place, the wrong time. Being a nature-lover, she knew this well.

And yes, she did often venture to the wrong places, often got lost. She never learnt. Regularly, she just set off without even telling anyone too. Independent, free, that could be why she was here. The flora and fauna of Celestia had always fascinated her, she had been truly mesmerised by what she could discover, by the array of life teeming out there. Especially in the barely trodden paths and woodland. She went off with her binoculars, notebook, and sketching pencils, observing insects, birds, small scurrying creatures, the larger field animals, and fierce predators. The whole circle of life on Celestia captivated her, like a spell. Being part of it, well it made her feel alive.

Jess could sit for hours, sometimes even a couple of days, just watching. There were so many peaceful and serene places on Celestia, especially in the land above Hallowed Brook. A vastness, full of beauty. Of course, you had to look beyond the pollution, the scarred areas where the land had been ravaged and the largely overpopulated residential towns which were closer to the Capital Core.

Jess knew that they were lucky in Hallowed Brook, that their homes amongst the tree canopy were so much better than the sprawling, skyline splitting tower blocks over in Divine City. Or the ugly squat brown bungalows, that twisted in haphazard rows and rows, like brooding rats across Sublime Town. Their homes were amongst nature, by the endless fields, intwined within the tall trees. They had the benefit of being at one with the creatures. She often just sat there, with Blue, staring into the woods, taking in the glory of life.

For a moment, the thought hit her like a fist in the guts.

She missed Blue, she missed her home. Would she ever see it again?

Her fingers traced the lines, the marks of four downward strokes and one across. The patterns that reflected both her strength and her sadness.

Deep within her, she knew it was important to remain optimistic, she needed to keep positive, she continually chastised herself within her head, within her heart. If her spirit was crushed, then they would sense it. It was just the way of the land. Jess had observed enough animals to know that she needed desperately to not give up. The minute you gave up, the animals that lurked in the shadows would pounce. She knew that she'd be history. That her bones would be left for the scavengers.

She had an inkling that this could be connected to what she had discovered. The buried secret that burned amongst the folds of her mind. But, surely no one knew. Knowing the magnitude, she had kept it all to herself, even if the searing sensation roiling within her brain had meant that she wanted to pass on some of the heat. Her mind pictured the truck, the machines.

A shadow fell over her as one of *them* suddenly appeared as if summoned by her thoughts. They tossed her a tray of food, not caring that some of the slop had hit the stony floor.

Without a word, red pulsing, they turned and left.

Jessie was glad it was dark. She was glad no one could see her burning humiliation. Her hands and feet were loosely bound so she had no option but to shuffle like a worm and eat from the plate with just her mouth. Like an animal.

Still, she thought, she'd rather be an animal than as low as these Droids.

Her captors were faceless machines that lacked any ounce of humanity. Celestians had made them, but they had failed to give them any positive human traits. Her silent captors were just expressionless, emotionless Droids and they were no doubt just blindly following orders.

She had gotten a good look at at least one of them before they had placed the hood over her head. It was only a split second, but it was enough. Enough to know that she has seen their kind before. Enough to realise why. Jess prided herself on being observant and she had sketched the robotic creature's likeness in her mind's eye.

Matt-black, featureless with a red laser that slunk back and forth across where their eyes should be. A malevolent, rhythmic pulse. Two thick mechanical arms, two sturdy mechanical legs. Strong and heavy. These Droids, when they spoke, communicated using excellent vocabulary. Their speech patterns were indistinct from Celestian's voices. The sound was eerie coming from a thick, matt-black peg doll.

They reminded Jess of the artists' dummies she'd seen once. They had been used in an art workshop in the Capital Core. Rich kids there were learning how to draw the form of Celestia's people, the class was about representing movement and posture. The art teacher had been enthusiastically moving the small wooden doll about whilst droning on about some Celestia artist's portfolio.

Jess and Blue had looked on from behind the glass window. Another time, months later, they'd delivered a dozen boxes of foraged beets, root vegetables and protein burgers to the college.

Apparently, there was some huge, elegant party that evening. A party for the rich donors who gave their money in order to have buildings named after them.

"Enjoy your worm burgers suckers," the girls had repeated all the way home. They had said it in different voices. Cracking up into fits of breathless laughter each time one of them cackled it.

Jess had been surprised when they had been chosen to do the Capital Core delivery run later in the same week, she was sure their hysterical tales would mean someone else was chosen.

Jessie shivered. That had been the first day that she had seen them. The things she wished she hadn't. The things that may have led her here: trussed up like a meat joint and eating off the floor. It was the first day she had seen the Droids too. Bile rose in her throat again.

Hell, she needed to get out.

As was her routine, she ate and slept and talked. She told Blue every little detail inside her head. She rabbited on like they were sat in the snug wooden chairs on one of their treehouse balconies. Like they were whispering conspiratorially in the inky-black night. Those perfect nights where they'd stayed up late, lanterns flickering, their giggles filling the Brook. How they'd tried hard not to wake the Hallowed Brook elders.

She had decided to tell Blue what she had seen. Like she should have done back then. If she'd revealed the truth of the terrifying thing that froze her blood and made her doubt her own sanity, perhaps she could have saved herself, saved the place she loved. So, she talked. Inside her head she recounted it all, right from the very start.

When she was done, she fell into a dream filled nightmare.

CHAPTER 4

THE VISIONARY

Titus Cariad stared up at the inky, dark skies and felt the rhythm of the planet beneath his bare feet. The endless hum and throb of the land. The energy of the soil vibrated up through his enormous body to his thick, bald head. The ancient stone he stood upon infused him with Celestia's higher power. Titus raised his arms up to the heavens and breathed deeply, a cleansing breath. Something swam in his lilac eyes. Worry. Something was off kilter. Something was wrong. Something was coming. He sensed a wisp of deep change. It unnerved him.

Titus focused on one tiny, twinkling dot high above, as he tried to empty his mind. Through the starlight and silence, he tried to summon up a vision. His lilac eyes closed, and he wanted to see. Every time he reached the twisting tendrils of his brain towards the prophecy, they fell flat.

All he felt was a deep overwhelming dread. A black, creeping landslide of dread.

Feeling a knot of frustration at his brow, he tried again. This time he allowed his inner thoughts to weave and meander. Perhaps, he could catch the tendrils of what was coming if he allowed his mind to flow like the thundering of The Great River far beyond this valley, across to the Western lands.

A coil of black, a snakelike twisting ribbon, slunk through his consciousness and up into his mind. It barred the truth, blocking the knowledge he sought. The coil spat and hissed whenever the details of the vision came too close, when he was within touching distance of what the vision was trying to tell him. He sighed with frustration. This strange entity seemed to be defending his mind, keeping out the details he sought. But was it guarding him or guarding the information? Titus Cariad, a man of learning, a man of answers, a man of The Oracle, he couldn't be sure.

This shouldn't be happening.

It was most unusual. In all his years as Visionary, he had never felt so blocked. He shuddered and tried to keep his giant body open. To channel the fragments of the future. He desperately tried to evict the snakelike blackness from his mind.

Mother Celestia
The one who
Provides
Open my eyes
Unlock my
Mind
Give me
Foresight
To work to
Your will
Send me
The light

So, I may be
Visionary still.

Perhaps the incantation might work, Titus mused as he parroted the familiar words. He realised angrily though, that that was what he was doing. He was merely repeating the praising prayer with no feeling. The coiling blackness was all he could think about. It consumed him. He was revering Mother Celestia with vacuous, empty words.

Annoyed with himself, feeling unnerved by the sense of things being askew, he said the divine words again. This time giving each syllable the gravitas it required. Titus now ensured that he meant every word.

Still the vicious black snake hissed. It morphed into a bat that flew in front of his eyes, blinding him.

Was he losing his powers?

This had never happened. Never in documented history. The Visionary was meant to be the one who saw the prophesies, each and every prophecy until his last breath.

Was it that he was dying?

Perhaps the snake, the bat, whatever it was, was here to take him to The Afterlands. Was it a portent of his passage to the life beyond? An omen.

The giant stamped his ebony, carved pole into the ground. His Visitotem, the twenty-foot staff, merely jolted in his large hand. There was no lightning flash, no rumble from beneath the soil, no blasted vision.

Could this be his final day?

A rare occurrence followed, Titus Cariad walked weakly back to his wooden shelter feeling flat and old.

His one hundred- and thirty-three-year-old bones creaked with each heavy step.

He was met by the roaring fire and Ryoni, his faithful companion. A four legged, waggy-tailed, wolfish creature, who was far more ball of soft wool, than fierce wolf. These guard hounds were known as Shadow wolves, and they had been domesticated, years back, from their larger, more vicious cousins: Hoarfrost Wolves.

The quizzical bark echoed around the valley. Ryoni seemed to sense his master's despondency. He rubbed his flank against The Visionary's legs, pulling playfully at his ornamental vestments. Ryoni's teeth snagged on The Visionary's Celestia sash. In slow motion, the midnight blue, decorated fabric unspooled in a long, winding stream. A galaxy imploding and scattering.

"Away! Quit it Ryoni, stop that, stop it now," Titus Cariad bellowed at the beast. He was taking his frustration out on the Shadow Wolf, and he knew it. Ryoni cowered, his amber eyes unsure.

He balled the Celestia sash in his hands and threw it at the cabin wall. The flames of his large, open fire made patterns dance on the walls.

Titus wasn't scared of dying. He knew a more sacred life awaited. The life beyond, his spiritual ever after. He had lived a long, fruitful existence. But recently, he had started to doubt, to fear. A myriad of murmurings constantly flittered around his head like unsettled birds. Titus had started to question the ancient texts and what they promised believers. He was losing his faith a little, becoming jaded. He rubbed his hand across his huge, hairless brow.

Tonight, had cemented that niggling doubt. He didn't like the disorientating sensation this had brought.

"Stop whining Ryoni!"

Titus suddenly felt incensed with rage; like he was aflame inside and not with the fervour of a believer.

The Shadow Wolf sat down in front of him with another quizzical look upon its furry face. It tilted its golden head to the side. Its floppy ears dangled down.

The Shadow Wolf whimpered.

"Ah Ryoni, you're hardly going to scare off the Heartstealer looking like that, are you?" Titus muttered. "I'm not going to be able to count on you to save me from The Wander. I'm not, am I?"

According to The Celestia Scrolls, The Heartstealer visited just before death to steal the hearts of non-believers. If it succeeded, it meant that they were forever doomed to The Wander. Skirting the plains between Celestia and The Afterlands. A place full of fear. A lonely forever after, that the people of Celestia tried to avoid at all costs. He would rather burn in the fires of Sinestre.

Titus was shocked by a shrill Ryoni bark.

Why was he so damned skittish tonight? Maybe this really was the end?

"Well, I might as well get us a decent last supper, eh?" Titus said to the unsettled mutt as he paced in front of the fire.

As he put together some food for the pair of them, he noticed his hands were shaking. He raised a hand up to his face to look more closely at the tremors. But his thoughts were interrupted by a loud, urgent knock upon his cabin door.

The Visionary sensed trouble.

CHAPTER 5

BLUE

Blue pottered around her small treehouse enjoying the birdsong, the peace and the sun's gentle rays.

Her sore neck and tense back still felt like they were made of lead, but as she bathed in the abundance of nature, she allowed herself to fully slow down. Blue sipped herb tea, ate fresh vegetable soup and read her favourite poetry books.

It was a long time since she had fully committed to her own needs. Blue was always running around, always busy, always helping other people out. This thing with Jessie had made her realise that, occasionally, you had to be selfish. She intended to make the most of this sick day.

The light dappled across her small sitting area, and she could smell the sweet, earthy tang of Valerian, it grew among the rocky outcrops nearby, in the valley where the treehouses had been built. The walls of billion-year-old rock provided a shelter from any fierce weather, and positioning their houses amongst the trees meant they didn't have to scrabble about in the thick, squelchy dirt.

Jessie's treehouse was mere metres from Blue's. They were joined by a rope bridge. The women had often laughed that they were so connected to each other that they needed a bridge to limit their time apart.

Blue glanced at Jessie's place now. She realised that she'd even been avoiding looking over that way. She'd found it too painful. The sight of the empty shelter made her grief seem enormous, hostile and threatening.

The shadowy treehouse represented her unfathomable loss, and it was made more poignant by the fact that she was continually connected to it, she couldn't escape it.

She glanced down at the anthology of poetry upon her lap. Her eyes properly focused on the words of the poem. The book had blown in a slight breeze and had come to rest on pages that she hadn't recalled reading before. It was an old poem, one from the fishermen of The Great River and The Azure Sea.

Struggle

Struggle
To stay buoyant
With each wave
Of crashing
Crushing power
That forces
A weakened
Listing vessel
Against unyielding
Rocks.

Flounder
Once elegantly
Navigating
Aquamarine seas

Iridescently bright
Sails sure
Course clear
Laughter mingling
With a tender
Breeze.

Depend
On the ballast
Deep below
There for
Times like these
A safety
Recognising
Storms subside
Morph into joyous
Blue.

Steady
Trust in the cycle
Head raised
To the horizon
Allow the dips
The plummets
Dark unknowns
Knowing soon
Spring ushers
Revival.

The poem's words were relevant, beautifully crafted, and they resonated deeply. Tears welled in her eyes. Blue was on the edge. Three months of pain seemed to pour from her in an unrelenting cascade. The tears stained the pages of the book. Large drops soaking through the paper, pitter pattering on the wooden floor.

Her struggle had been largely alone. Troy and Ky missed Jessie too, but they were convinced that she'd return. Blue was tired of holding in her hurt, these words seemed to open locked floodgates. As if, the poetry had spoken to her soul. She wept unashamedly, letting the sadness spill from the book's pages, creating a pool upon the dusty floor.

After a short while, Blue remembered that Jessie sometimes wrote bits and pieces of poetry and, she had scrapbooked and journaled too. She'd not considered before that there could be some clues just sitting over there in the treehouse. Perhaps some of her notebooks or sketchbooks might tell them where exactly they should look. Where she could be.

Blue was adamant that they shouldn't just assume that she was coming back. Troy and Ky, like many others, thought that she would stroll back into the Brook as if nothing had happened. The whole village seemed sure that Jess was just off exploring.

For three months!

Blue realised that the evidence she needed, the evidence that may make people listen, to show that they needed to search for her instead, might be right there in her treehouse.

Blue put down her cup of herb tea, she wiped her crimson mottled pain-streaked face. Looking towards the bridge, she stood, wincing as a lightning bolt of agony struck.

Damned back.

Before she crossed, at the threshold, she hesitated just for a moment. She had an eerie sense of unease.

Would this just make her feel worse? Make the pain far more intense? Render the small amount of healing and adjustment useless. Put her right back to square one.

Her head felt as if it were buried in dirt. It felt thick with an overwhelming, muffled confusion. Everything was slow, slightly off kilter, echoey.

"I need to go in there, I need to," Blue said aloud making Scruffy, her black and white Treecat, jump from his sleeping spot with a look of alarm. His fur stood on end as if he'd been electrified.

"Sorry buddy," Blue murmured. "Just talking to myself again."

Ignoring her screaming back, dreading what she would see, hoping to find a clue, Blue crossed the bridge into Jessie's treehouse.

Everything was covered in a thick layer of dirt. Dust really, three months of dust. Here though, the dust was dark, like ashes. The table in the corner was still set for breakfast, a colourful teapot sat next to a polka dot bowl.

As Blue tiptoed closer, the hairs on her neck rising, she saw a chaos of insects feasting on what was left inside. They swarmed, enjoying the feast. She flinched and let out a small, muted scream. She needed to get a grip.

They're tiny girl and you pick them from the dirt every day!

Jessie's teasing words, as always, rang strident in her mind.

Blue entered the small bedroom. Photographs of them together, from the machines at The Capital Core, were tacked to the walls. The lump in her throat was dry, it made it hard to breathe. Hard to carry on.

There was an old, wooden Calete Company vegetable crate by Jessie's bed. Blue spotted the cheerful, colourful notebooks peeping from the pile of Jessie's odds and sods. Whenever they travelled to the Capital Core, she would buy an armful of books with coins that she had squirrelled away.

Blue took a deep breath, she had another urge to turn back, she needed to do this though. For Jess.

The circular bed was neat and tidy, so Blue pulled out a couple of scrapbooks and plonked herself down on the covers. She placed a rainbow-coloured cushion under her.

The first one she opened up was a riot of colour: words, pressed flowers, little drawings, verses. It was almost too much, a sob caught in her throat, and she almost began to cry again. The scrapbook seemed like a eulogy; Jessie's life laid out. Her blue eyes brimmed with tears making everything blurry.

But then she spotted something. It was a set of instructions, directions that led to a lake. Next to the directions Jess had drawn a small map. A cross marked a spot at the side of the shoreline.

When Blue looked closer, there was a scribble of words written in Jessie's looping, decorative hand. It was almost indecipherable. Blue willed the words to make sense.

"Cave tunnel? Is that what it says?" She said frustratedly.

She turned page after page, marvelling at the intricacies of the drawings: a Hornslant Snake in long grass, the side view of a Piper hound – a wild dog with a long thin snout and a whiplike tail.

There were little rhymes, more pressed petals, small feathers and descriptions of the weather. Jess had sketched small birds, collected colourful pebbles. Blue marvelled at the icicles she had drawn, the shading was so perfect that they could almost be real. The Devout Drolle soared in the sky above a mountain ridge.

The scrapbooks were like a sensory journey through Jessie's passions. Blue had been out with her a few times, but her spinal problems in recent years, meant that she hadn't found the longer treks much fun. Blue was now more of a home bird. She loved to read, losing herself in epic myths and legends, in tales of kings and queens, of magical sorcerers and plots to invade kingdoms. Poetry too entranced her. Whilst Jess saved to buy scrapbooks, art materials, Blue spent her coins in the Capital Core bookshops.

Now she could see what she had been missing: the story of Celestia's vast natural beauty was emerging in front of her eyes. It was like an intrepid trip into the unknown. It drew her in.

A shrill shriek spooked her, and she dropped the book with a start. It tumbled to the tree house floor as her heart pounded. It was a Howler Crake, a bird that had a distinctive, terrifying mating call.

Damn it.

Blue leant down to retrieve the book. Something had fallen out of the back. A folded, aged piece of paper. The paper looked as if it might disintegrate if she touched it; it was tissue thin and discoloured. Blue picked it up gingerly.

Perhaps it was a love note, one Jess had kept since being young. Suddenly, this all felt wrong, like she was spying, disrespectful, an intrusion into Jessie's privacy. She wrestled with the feeling. But, this could also be integral to saving her life, to getting her friend back.

Slipping the scrapbooks and the ancient piece of paper into a cloth bag, she headed back across the bridge, returning to Scruffy. She really needed to speak to Ky.

As well as being Elysium Fields resident heartthrob, Ky was also a collector. He bought and sold artefacts from the past from a small shack. His trading post. He would know how to handle this piece of delicate paper without damaging it. She would pass by his treehouse or see if he was over in his shack as soon as he was back from the forage.

Mesmerised by the detail and vibrancy of Jessie's scrapbooks, Blue curled up on her own bed, slowly turning the pages. She tried to commit as much of what she saw to memory. As much as was possible, to see if anything could point to ways of locating Jessie.

A short verse stood out.

I am the wanderer
With the eyes of
A child
But in a heartbeat
What forms
Terrifies me.

There was a strange sketch next to the lines. Instead of the natural drawings, the insects, birds, flowers, Jess had sketched a building. A large concrete block with barred windows. At the windows she had drawn a group of long faces. Instead of eyes though, these faces had a red slit, like a bloody gash.

A creeping feeling of jittery unreality coursed around Blue's veins and her stomach seemed to somersault. Who the hell were the figures in the drawing? Did they have anything to do with Jess going missing? Why did the building look so familiar?

A skittery, spider-like memory twitched in her brain but stayed just out of reach.

Yes, she really needed to speak to Ky.

CHAPTER 6

TROY

An icy chill made Troy's scalp feel tight across his skull and a shiver snaked down his spine. The visit to The Visionary filled him with anxiety, but he didn't know what else to do.

Troy came from a long line of farmers. They'd created a settlement here and worked the land here for centuries. Before the pox had wiped the beasts out, they'd raised woolly sheep, spiny hogs and pasture cows. Good, nutritional food.

Now, they planted whatever vegetables they could into the cracked and unyielding soil, rounded up worms and insects from the boggy ground instead of rounding cattle, and tried to produce enough nutritional material to feed some of Celestia's population.

Keeping livestock was no longer an option. Over the years, too many diseases had passed from the beasts they kept for food. Viruses that were catastrophic for the people. Contagious, fast-spreading viruses had wiped out a big chunk of Celestia's population. It had been heartbreaking, so much death.

So, they relied on vegetables and worms. It was a dirty job, a job that required grit and gumption, it was his inheritance. A ball and chain that felt heavier than his young shoulders could support. Calete Company was now a large business trying to deal with the Capital Core's food demands.

He sighed. Sometimes his legacy felt like a tightening noose around his neck.

His father, Terrence, once a proud, stoic man, was sick now. He had become weak after the pox had obliterated most of the family's livestock. Troy knew that his close proximity to the animals made it highly likely that he would catch something one day. But they hadn't realised how destructive it would be. He'd been ravaged by the effects of Spiny Pig Pox, wept as he had slaughtered and burnt the pigs he had raised. He'd never recovered. And, for Troy, life was never the same again.

Terrence Calete had reluctantly passed the work to his boy. He'd had little choice in the giving, and Troy had had little choice in the accepting. It was just the way. The way of the land, the way of Celestia. His aunt, Eliza, now held the reins and Troy worked to ensure the fields were run properly, checking that the foragers gleaned as much as they could from the dirt. His father had been sent away to a place where he could receive healing.

Visionaries were giants that lived amongst the ridges of the mountain, each area of land had their own. They were very important to those who toiled daily upon the land. They could warn of dangerous weather, predict crop failures and diseases, see any obstacles that may stand in the way of producing enough food. The giants communicated with the many spirits of the heavens.

The Visionary was tied into the core beliefs of the people who lived around and about. The spirits of the air, water, earth, metal and fire, passed messages from their gods, these elementals spoke through him. It was to The Visionary that many people turned in times of crisis.

Still, Troy feared the enormous, old sage. Feared what he might say, feared that he would see the secrets that Troy kept buried. The dirt in his family's past. He wanted advice but he didn't want to say too much. Anything that would put someone else in danger.

Hearing a wolf's ragged howl, raising himself up tall, he knocked again. The huge ornate door was worn down by years of sun, rain, wind, and visitors. It creaked open with a shuddering groan. Troy stood peering up into the face of the ancient soothsayer, his heart in his mouth.

The giant's enormous bald head and piercing lilac eyes materialised out of the gloom. Troy shrank back, he fought the urge to run. The Shadow Wolf, as tall as Troy's chest, sniffed the air and bared its teeth. Troy took a defensive step backwards.

"You standing out there in the gloaming or you coming in?" The old giant's strident tone rang in the evening air. Troy gulped.

"Well?" The Visionary raised one of his meaty hands in a questioning gesture, as he opened the cabin door wider still, revealing the log fire within.

"Cat got your tongue boy?" Came the half-chuckled prod.

"No... I mean yes...I mean, yes, I'm coming in Visionary, thank you."

The room smelt of concoctions, of potions and incense. It was homely, the flickering firelight mesmerising. It had been a long time since Troy had needed to light a fire. But, after trekking upwards through the frigid air it was a welcome sight. The flames danced in a hypnotic, rhythmic twist and Troy was drawn towards the hearth.

"Sit boy," The Visionary muttered.

Calling him boy rankled. The wolf eyed him with suspicion, its hackles were raised, its belly close to the floor. A strange position that stretched the beast out of kilter.

Troy felt his heart flutter rapidly, abruptly he sat, following the Visionary's orders. Once his bottom hit the base of the large stool, he blew out a loud breath. A breath that he hadn't even realised that he was holding. Titus Cariad eyed him curiously. Troy felt a wave of anxiety, like he was back in lessons, learning his A B Cs. Finding out how to add and subtract, he felt like he was peering up at someone who knew everything whilst he knew nothing.

"I know who you are," The visionary began. "I know your father and knew his father. I even knew the father of your grandfather. So, tell me boy, why are you here?"

Troy gulped suddenly feeling foolish, out of his depth. Like the boy that Titus saw in him. Why was he here? He desperately tried to fathom which bits of information he should reveal, what he should instead keep to himself. Troy knew this train of thought was ultimately foolish. Titus Cariad knew everything.

"Boy, I can read you. You want to know if I know why she's missing. Or if I know what it is that she saw. You know things…don't you Troy son of Terrence?," Titus Cariad's voice was like an incantation, melodic. His face clouded over, his huge form seemed to ebb and flow in the fire's light. The giant's lilac eyes seemed to bore into Troy's very soul, seeing into the core of him. His head felt fuzzy, the smells overpowered him, the heat of the roaring fire made him feel faint. What did he mean? Half the words made no sense. The silence stretched.

For a long time, The Visionary remained silent, peering. The wrinkled brown skin of his huge arms tensed. He clasped his hands in front of him as if in prayer. The air felt charged.

"Tell me everything Troy Calete, leave nothing out, you must tell me everything you know."

The Shadow Wolf howled.

CHAPTER 7

JESS

She awoke with a start, gasping for air. The memories of that day, the horror of what she had been involved in, the path that had led her here, twisted like wisps of choking black smoke, blurring reality. It took her a while to remember where she actually was.

The cave was quiet as the incessant dripping seemed to have temporarily ceased. Listening, she tried to figure out if her captors were about. There were no discernible sounds, and she took that as a good sign. Light flooded in through a crevice high above her. She welcomed the glow. Last night, Jess had managed to free her left arm and the relief of now having a limb to prop herself up was keeping her going. It was a start. If she focused, perhaps she could escape this place. She'd wriggled free before, but they'd always noticed and tightened her tethers. This time, she wanted to keep her freedom a secret.

To distract herself, she picked up a small rock and began to scratch patterns in the smooth parts of the cave floor. Before she knew it she was drawing the Droids. Finding an even smaller piece of rock, shaped almost like a pencil, she added words.

Black outer shell.

Red laser eye.

Normal speech.

At home, sketching and scrapbooking soothed her mind, so for the first time in three months the cacophony of questions, the anger, the tension... everything began to fade. She became lost in her drawings, recording in pictures and words her current reality. She'd seen them before, sketched them before, but now she knew their true significance. The significance of what they meant for the land.

From her memory, she drew a map of the area they had taken her from and, believing she was in caves below some mountains, she scratched an impression of the location. She knew they had travelled North because the setting sun had been on her right-hand side. Celestia's sun set in the East. She used the stone to draw the sand dunes they had crossed, the second lake they had skirted around with the purple tinged water. She drew the fork in the road where they had taken the right path upwards. The things she had managed to see before they had placed the hood over her head. She was lost in her own world, making marks, recording her trauma, indelibly scratching it into the stone.

A loud clatter shocked her and the rock she had been using rolled out of reach.

They were bringing food. Jessie's stomach rumbled emptily. It may be slop, but it was keeping her alive, and the patterns she had carved into the stone had energised her, given her hope. One day she might live to tell her tale, to properly record what had happened in one of her scrapbooks. She lay down, covering the marks on the stone with her body, making sure to hold her arm as if it was still bound. Shivering, she awaited the tray.

As the strange Droid dropped down the food, Jess clung onto this renewed hope as a lifeline. She had to stay alive. She had to get out. She had to get home, back to Blue.

***

Jess continued etching patterns on the stone floor, and then up upon the walls of the cave, late into the night. Through the high up crevice, she could see the stars. Despite her circumstances, that slice of sky was mesmerising.

With determination, she had managed to partially free her other arm. The bonds, she realised, were beginning to weaken in the damp, the cords becoming spongy and frayed. She found she could stand. Her feet were still bound but the ties were much looser.

Stretching up, feeling the most like herself than she had felt in months, she stared up at the twinkling pinpricks of faraway light. Jess listened to the rhythmic pattern of her exerted breathing, the echoes of the cave, the faint sounds that came to her through the crevice. Still now, she calmed her mind.

She wondered if someone out there was feeling the same way she did. Was another woman up there, alone in the dark, staring up into the light of the heavens, looking at the other planets, desperately wracking her brains for a way to return home?

The meagre light was momentarily blocked. The huge, elegant body of a Devout Drolle flashed above her cave. Its golden beak shimmered in the moonlight; it's feathers like twirling, twisting flames. Free. Then, in the blink of an eye it had gone. Off riding the thermals, swooping on the winds, diving then soaring.

Jessie breathed in the air, thought about the wonderfully enchanting bird, then she whispered the words out into the bitter night. Her intentions caught on the ribbons of darkness trailing in the air, they flew forever upwards, pausing before twirling amongst the starlight.

> *Another life awaits me*
> *To it I will rise*
> *Be free as the forest creatures*
> *That scurry and fly.*

She missed being able to write poetry, to draw, to make sense of her world through her scrapbooks. One day she wanted to write about this experience, to free herself of the trauma. She knew she would survive this, be free again, she was filled with steely fortitude.

CHAPTER 8

THE VISIONARY

By the glowing embers of the fire, The Visionary listened to the tale of Troy Calete, realising, with each word uttered, that there was a shift occurring.

He furtively looked towards his Visitotem, but the tall staff was still, unchanged.

Titus had to try hard to keep his imposing face straight. The temptation to ruffle his forehead, widen his eyes and gape in disbelief, was strong. It would be wrong to do so, the spirits would not approve. But as the tale became more tangled, the layers of murkiness mounting up to a point that even he couldn't believe the web of secrets, he found himself struggling to keep his moon-like face nonchalant.

Whilst he was glad that the young man had come to him, he felt irritated with the heavy burden of the revelations, that made his heart sink. This was his role. Titus could see the man needed help, guidance, reassurance from the spirits, but there was an overwhelming urge to throw him out, to bolt the door and bury the echoes of his words in a place where they would never again be heard. He knew he couldn't abandon his responsibility though.

Ryoni whined and paced. Whined and paced. The hound also deeply unsettled. His faithful companion kept nudging at Titus' hand as Troy spoke, as if urging him to take action. But this was his vocation, the way that had been chosen for him, the path that he walked. Troy, the young man in front of him, didn't seem to understand the significance of half of his words. The things he was revealing and how they linked to other murky problems. He was clueless, ranting without joining any dots. No clue about the Pandora's box he was opening on this star filled night. Despite this, Titus was overwhelmed with a sense of unease, the weight of which he had never felt before in his long life.

As the story came to a close, he sat almost frozen. A cough, from the young man, finally shook him from his inertia.

"Boy, the way forward for you has not materialised at this time. It is shrouded still. I must mull over this, seek signs from the spirits. What you have revealed is bigger than this realm, much bigger. I'm sorry that I do not have a clear path for you to take. What you have spoken of tonight, it may have tremors, aftershocks that will be felt beyond Celestia. Let it be known, I will need to speak to you again."

The young man looked disheartened. His face, in that fleeting moment, like that of a much older man, double his years. The strain seemed to be taking a heavy toll upon him. Troy Calete appeared more confused than when he had first arrived. That wouldn't do.

"Is there a way for me to find some temporary peace? A spell, a potion, some ritual that I can perform?"

Troy asked, his eyes filled with a pleading desperation. "Please Visionary. I need some way to seek relief from the continual sense of unease?"

The Visionary wracked his brains for something that might comfort him. He looked at Ryoni and an idea began to materialise.

"I hear you boy. Fear not, Troy son of Terrence, for there is a way to earn the favour of those who sit in judgement," he continued. "Before I seek guidance from the spirit world in relation to your tale, you must display your remorse here in the physical realm. Find an animal in need and care for it, a gesture that demonstrates your commitment to healing. To setting things right."

There was a long silence as Troy digested The Visionary's words.

As they sat by the fire, within the mountains of Celestia, in the valley below the towering Astral Peak, Titus Cariad, looked at Troy Calete with a gaze that seemed to pierce the fabric of time itself. The Visionary closed his eyes and breathed deeply, feeling the pulse of the world and the currents of destiny intertwine.

"Know boy, this is just a step," intoned The Visionary, his voice resonating with the wisdom of ages. "Redemption is a path woven with deeds of healing and contrition. You have a chance boy. Embrace it."

Troy's gaze remained fixed on the giant, his voice betraying a mixture of desperation and confusion. "But Titus, how can this help to make amends?"

The Visionary extended a hand, motioning out toward the valley, to the expanse of the world around them.

"In Celestia's complex creation, every creature plays a role. Seek out an animal in need, one whose life you can safeguard and nurture. Let this act be a testament to your sense of what is right. I will help boy, I assure you. This show of compassion will be a ribbon, threads of a larger, entwined tapestry that will tell a tale of the man you truly want to be. The man who inhabits your future."

"An animal? Does it have to be a specific kind?" Troy spluttered, clearly taken aback by the unexpected request.

"I feel that, with patience, the creature may very well find you Troy son of Terrence."

Ryoni howled loudly, the startling noise reverberating up into the mountains and filling the valley.

Troy Calete, his face grave. He didn't have a clue.

CHAPTER 9

BLUE

In the dappled light of the forest, under Ky's treehouse. Blue clasped Jessie's scrapbook to her chest as she tentatively approached her friend's makeshift trading post. Ky was not in his tree house, so he must be here. The ground had hardened a little, but the journey across the sodden fields had fatigued her. She tried to release some tension, lowering her shoulder blades and concentrating on relaxing her neck and back muscles.

The afternoon air was tinged with anticipation as she glanced inside Ky's treasure trove. The door was ajar, and she eyed the eclectic array of curiosities and relics that surrounded him. Blue took a deep breath, sure that this was an important step towards finding her friend. She looked up to the sky before she crossed the threshold, her blue eyes searching for a sign. She saw only angry clouds.

Ky's eyes were lowered as he tinkered with a tiny silver clock. The delicate heirloom was shimmering in the light, it's jewelled dial captivating, and Blue smiled at how engrossed Ky was as he used tweezers to tease open the mechanism. She stood silent for a moment, unwilling to disturb him. This was a side of the boisterous, playful Ky that only a few ever got to see. His tongue slipped between his lips; his forehead furrowed with deep concentration.

With a wide smile that mirrored her own, he noticed her, beckoning for her to come closer.

"Come in, I'm not long back from the fields. How's the pain?"

"Ky," she began, her voice carrying a mixture of excitement and urgency. "I found something in Jess's scrapbook. It's a fragment of an old map, it was tucked away, hidden at the back, I found the scrapbook in a crate inside her treehouse. I don't know why I hadn't looked in there before." The words came out in a garbled burst, as butterflies danced around her stomach, their wings teasing and tickling her insides. Blue was sure that this map was important.

"Whoa…whoa whoa…slow down Blue… start again. Scrapbooks…a map you say?"

Ky's attention was definitely piqued. He laid a cloth over the silver clock, setting it to one side almost immediately. With care, he moved another tray, filled with antiquities, his eyes narrowing with curiosity as he repeated her words.

"So, there was a map hidden in the back of a scrapbook. That's what you found?"

Blue nodded, offering him the book and the delicate map with a tremble of trepidation. Could this be a turning point in the riddle of Jessie's disappearance?

Ky's large, rough hands handled the pages with delicate precision, with gentle care. Blue watched as he marvelled at the images that Jess had sketched, just like she had done. His brown eyes flickering over the words. He trailed his gaze eagerly over the items she had pressed into the pages. Blue found herself entranced again, she held her breath as he ran his fingertips gently over the feather of an Opal eagle, and touched a tiny, pink spiral fossil. After scrutinising the pages with fascination, his breath caught in his throat as he turned to the map. She watched with wonder as his skilled fingers caressed the aging paper. As he used slender silver tongs to carefully open the fragment of the old map, he ensured that no tear marred its surface. It was a slow, steady process. The air was filled with a palpable hope.

Before their eyes, the map unfurled, revealing a landscape that was simultaneously familiar and foreign. Ky's brows furrowed as he examined the marks upon the aged parchment. His weighty magnifying glass, with the mahogany handle and golden trim, helped him to scrutinise the small details much more closely.

"I recognise parts of this," he mused aloud. "But some sections are blurred, like they've been deliberately obscured."

Blue's gaze remained fixed on the landscape that was being revealed within the map. Her chest heaved with unspoken words. She decided to share her concerns.

"Ky, I think Jess saw something she shouldn't have," she said, her voice laced with the weight of her worry. "There are hints in her scrapbook that point to secrets she may have uncovered."

"Secrets… what kind of secrets?" Ky murmured as he read a snippet of verse that jumped out at him. A couple of bold lines from one of the drawing-filled pages.

Dirt is where we begin
And where we end
But what if the dirt

Is tainted?

"Dirt, hmmm…I guess we spend far too long digging in it, do you think that's what she meant here?"

"I don't know. I'm unsure of what half of this really means to be honest with you Ky. But, something is off."

He paused, his brown eyes rising to meet hers, before he pored over more of the pages.

"Blue, how do you fancy a trek? I think perhaps we should take a few days off and see if we can find anything out there. Out where she used to roam. Search for any signs or clues. I hadn't really though about it before, but…. I feel we need to. We owe it to Jess."

Blue's heart began to pound rapidly, a flicker of possibility ignited deep within her core as her tense throat constricted. This is what she had hoped for. At last.

Ky's adventurer's spirit seemed further ignited as he traced his fingers mesmerizingly over the map's contours. She could see the cogs twisting and turning, this way and that, in his mind.

"I think we need to follow the clues," he declared, his eyes alight with the thrill of the unknown. "I know this, this spot here, look it's Lumina Lake, see? There's the lake here on the map just below the mountains. That's the Atlas Peak high up in the Desire range. It's a long trek, further than I've ever ventured, hours away, but I've heard of it. And, if it was up to me, then that's where I believe we should start. We might find answers, some kind of clues. Some sort of sign to her whereabouts could very well lie hidden near here."

Blue beamed up at him, she was elated, she'd hoped and prayed for this reaction, but still, Blue felt a little unsure.

"Ky, it's a long journey. We can't just rush into this," she breathed. "We need to involve Troy, to let him know, he won't just want us to take off. The quotas…the fields. I'm wondering what we should tell him, about Jess and the map. About a trek out to this lake." Her voice quivered with feelings of caution.

Ky's grin softened as he glanced sheepishly at his friend.

"You're right," he mused. "He's the boss after all. We need to be careful, thorough; we might be gone for hours, a day or two even, and he'll worry. Let's tell Troy about Jessie, the scrapbook, and the map. Then, together, we'll decide if we should go out there."

The air grew suddenly colder as the sun began to dip below the horizon. Blue shuddered and wrapped her arms around herself, it would be bitter in the mountains. She glanced at Ky as they stood, filled with dreams, amidst the relics of the past. It was clear that they shared a desire to do what they could to uncover the truth, that they both had a need for answers. Blue knew that they held a fragile chance in their hands, that they had an opportunity and an obligation to unravel the tangled threads of Jessie's disappearance. The stumbling block, the obstacle would be Troy.

Within the pages of Jessie's scrapbook and the fragment of the old map, little did they know that they held the complex chords of a mystery that had the potential to unravel deep, twisted secrets of both the past and the present. A mystery that threatened the future.

Unbeknown to Blue and Ky, they were watched as

they discussed how to approach Troy. Unseen eyes tracked them, alerting others of their findings. A red, pulsing sensor captured images and long-range listening devices recorded their excited, hushed conversations. A black hidden figure analysed their words.

The dirt was gathered, stored and secreted away.

CHAPTER 10

TROY

Troy left The Visionary's forest home with more questions than answers. He slowly headed back to the meadow listening to the many twitters, grunts and roars that defined the teeming natural wilderness around this part of Celestia. The place they called home. He was lost in thought as he trudged down towards the Brook, only partly realising that the night had almost slipped into day.

It was within the midst of this verdant landscape, with the sun awakening, softly lighting the sky, that Troy's heavy footsteps led him to an unexpected encounter. Unexpected but no doubt fated.

At first, he almost trampled over the beast, his head being so full of dark, murky thoughts. But, as its pitiful cries rang out, and it tried to flee, Troy stopped and investigated the tangled brambles and twisted vines that he was wading through. The roughly hewn path, a shortcut to the treehouses of their home. There, nestled among the foliage, lay an injured creature, a Lunafi. A small wild creature native to Celestia. Its coat, a blend of moonlit silver and deep indigo, was matted and stained, blood, from a deep, piercing wound, was visible, evidence of its struggle against some sort of predator. The tiny thing could barely move. Its torn foreleg appeared bent at a strange angle. As the sun rose, the injuries became clearer. Ordinarily, a creature such as this would scarper, run as soon as it heard the reverberating footsteps of someone's approach. It was rare for anyone to see them close up. They were skittish and nervy, terrified of their own shadows.

Troy's mind was filled with uncertainty as he gazed down at the wounded Lunafi. Doubt wrestled within him, but his thoughts eventually echoed The Visionary's words. The talk of a path of redemption through compassion and protection. With trembling, hesitant hands, he reached down towards the creature, his open palms a gesture of care, of surrender. He hoped the frightened creature wouldn't tear at his flesh with its razor-sharp claws, or worse, bite him with its needle fangs.

Sensing the animal's profound weakness, he became less concerned, less afraid of attack. The poor thing was clearly at death's door.

Gently, Troy scooped the injured Lunafi into his arms, the creature's body was warm against his skin, pleasant after the cold air of the upper valley. As he sensed its rapid heartbeat and heard its intermittent chirps and purrs, he felt a connection form, a link. A shared vulnerability that, in that frozen moment, seemed to transcend words.

The Lunafi's amber eyes, heavy with pain, met his gaze with a mixture of fear, pleading and need. The small, furry animal's bushy tail began to curl and twist. The movement was almost hypnotic.

Guided by the memory of The Visionary's words, Troy cradled the injured Lunafi tight against his chest, his steps carrying them toward his treehouse. As he walked, the rhythmic rise and fall of the creature's breathing became a sign. To Troy it was a sign of the fragility of life and the potential for healing. He hoped that this act could bring him some peace. He needed peace.

Arriving at his home within the canopy, Troy carefully climbed the rungs with the creature tucked into his shirt, then, immediately, he fashioned a makeshift basket bed of soft fabrics and blankets. With soft hands, he tended to the Lunafi's wounds, using gentle touch and soothing words to offer comfort. A balm, one used to ease the pain of nicked fingers and blistered feet, was smothered on the poor creature's wounds.

"Shhh little one, shhh now," Troy murmured.

He watched as the creature's breathing settled, its amber eyes now mirroring the sense of trust that had taken root in the pair of them.

He would need to find some food. For years, the people had avoided eating any creatures other than insects, worms and bugs. So, there was nothing suitable for a hungry carnivore in his treehouse. The risk of viruses being spread from eating the meat of other mammals was now too high. Perhaps the wild creature would eat some dried worm jerky.

But, when Troy looked down at the furry bundle, he discovered that the Lunafi was fast asleep. The sight brought him deep peace, the first sense of peace he had truly felt for weeks.

Troy was suddenly numb and exhausted. His eyes were heavy, and he had trouble keeping them open. His feet were sore from walking most of the night.

Picking up the basket that contained the lightly snoring wild animal, he moved across to his bed then fell on top of the cosy blankets, carefully placing the animal's basket beside him.

Within seconds, Troy had given in to the pull of deep, heavy slumber. His mind, for once still, his chest rising and falling in time with the silvery, purple Lunafi.

CHAPTER 11

JESS

She had almost taken a chance to escape today. Almost. In the end though, she had been too afraid of the peg-doll Droids tracking her down easily, of them killing her on the snowy mountain slopes, of her body lying motionless, for years, upon the ice.

She pictured it and it made her freeze in fear.

She knew it was biting cold, icy out there. The Droids had given her fur blankets, they had insisted on her covering herself after giving her a thick, woollen jumper to wear. They had seen her loosened tethers, but they hadn't seemed to care about that, or that she could see their faces, their forms. That worried her.

She'd watched the fascinating flakes as they'd slowly danced through the opening in the cave. The frosted filigree pattens had blown in the bitter breeze.

She'd had an idea then, as she had marvelled at the unique flakes twisting and tumbling at the whim of the wind, an idea to send a sign. A message to anyone who may be searching for her. And, surely, they would search...

Without too much thought, she roughly tore at the dress she was wearing. Ripping off a large piece by the hem. The thin cornflower-blue fabric, decorated with tiny yellow flowers was distinctive. Jess had made the dress herself; she wore it often. If people who knew her found a snippet of the fabric, they could maybe locate her.

Carefully, she tied the torn strip around a largish rock from the floor of the cave. Her numb fingers made tying the knot tricky. When it was finally secure, she half crouched, half stood below the opening in the cave's surface. With a forceful upward toss, she threw it out of the crevice. Her first attempt saw the rock tumbling straight back into the cave. Gritting her teeth in frustration, she bent to retrieve it. This time, she angled her throw, chucking the stone diagonally out.

The exertion exhausted her. Jess plonked back down on the fur blankets and hugged her arms around herself. She wondered if she could climb out of there. With some effort she thought she probably could, and, in a rush, she stood on her tiptoes, her hands grazing the stone rim. But the stone was needle sharp and jagged, her arms weak. It was far too high. Anguished, she slunk back down to the ground.

In the heart of the desolate cave, Jess's emotions ebbed and flowed like the changeable winds of Celestia. Hope and despair waged a silent battle within her, casting shadows and light across her weary spirit. With every passing moment, the walls seemed to close in, as the silence seemed to whisper a haunting tale of tragedy.

Yet, within the darkness, Jess found solace in the rock faces, in the drawings that adorned the cave walls. They were her companions, her silent testimony, and her artistic canvas. With skilled hands, she had sketched scenes of the world that she had known, each stroke of the stone a marker of her artistic skill and proof of her determined will to be back out, back in the light.

Drawings of Celestia's creatures danced alongside intricate maps, the lines a story script to the memories etched deep in her mind. Words woven with heartfelt intention filled the gaps, their letters forming bridges to the past, the present, and the uncertain future. In this labyrinth of despair, she had poured her waning energy, her boredom, her desire to distract her mind. Her fears too.

Jess gazed upon her creations now, tracing the fine lines towards the lower section, by her makeshift bed. She felt the indentations with her fingers as if reaching out to the world she so dearly missed. The creatures she had encountered in Celestia came alive through her sketches, their forms morphing from the mere strokes of a stone into living, moving beasts, shapes that often inhabited her dreams.

One word loomed large from the jumble of letters.

"Calete."

Wrapped in the warmth of fur blankets, Jess eventually surrendered herself to sleep again, to that realm where her mind could roam free and unburdened. Dreams carried her back to the landscapes she had once traversed, the rustling of leaves, the ploughed fields, the verdant canopy and the melodies of Celestia's creatures, were like a soothing lullaby.

With each breath, Jess clung to the images she had immortalised on the cave walls. They were her anchors now, her lifeline, and her reminder of the strong desire for freedom that burned bright within her. How she longed to be back with Blue.

In her vivid dreams, the world beyond the cave's confines beckoned, reminding her that even in the darkest of times, the spark of hope remained alive, leading the way to a future where the Celestia she longed for would once again embrace her with its magic, marvel and mystery.

She clutched at the wisps of her dream, allowing herself to be soothed. Taking comfort in the blanketing swirl of memories, dreams and conjured wishes.

CHAPTER 12

THE VISIONARY

S eated cross-legged within the stone crystal circle atop his rocky outcrop, The Visionary, Titus Cariad, contemplated the enigma of the missing woman, Jess. His mind was a swirling vortex of thoughts, Troy Calete's revelations mingled with the hazy, half revealed shadows of the Calete family's troubled history. In the embrace of the crystal circle, he sought clarity, a connection to the threads of the past and a link to the whispers of the future, to the wonders of the world of the spirits.

With his eyes closed, he delved deep, his mind reaching out, trying to take the tendrils of his own essence up into the expanse of Celestia's heavens, beyond the earthly realm, soaring up high. Yet, as he strained to summon forth a vision, the ethereal realm was elusive, slipping through his large grasp like fine pebbles, like gritty dirt.

A familiar presence padded next to him, his loyal Shadow Wolf, Ryoni, sat down heavily by his side. With an affectionate lick upon Titus Cariad's giant visage, the Shadow Wolf inadvertently scattered the precious crystals that adorned the circle, causing them to tumble and twinkle like fallen stars. The neat circle became a messy, haphazard maze and the link with the spirits was broken. He had to swallow down a shout of rage, a curse.

Exhaling a frustrated breath, The Visionary watched the scattered crystals glint against the ground, their reflections mirroring his feelings of inner turmoil. For a moment, irritation clouded his desire for guidance and he fought the urge to crush the crystals. This was becoming an annoyance. It was happening too often. He was, after all, The Visionary. Titus was the one chosen to harness the spirits, to unravel the tapestry of time, and offer guidance to those who sought it.

As he began to rearrange the crystals, his fingers deftly returning them to their rightful places, a sigh escaped his pursed lips. Doubt weighed upon his shoulders, and he questioned his own abilities once more. The snaking blackness coiled in his mind. Why had his visions forsaken him now when Jess's fate hung in the balance?

He feared the black snake that had tormented him the other day, he feared what it was trying to keep him from. He knew it was to do with the things Troy Calete had spoken of, of the murky secrets connected to The Calete family.

With a final attempt, he positioned each crystal carefully and reverently back in its sacred place, weaving the threads of energy once more. Willing his thoughts to a higher vibration. His thoughts intertwined with the melodies of the wind, and his plea echoed upwards, into the vast expanse above his rocky outcrop, then down into the valley.

And then, as if in response to his unwavering

determination, a single phrase echoed through the heavens, a whisper carried on the chilly breeze:

"Find Jess."

In that fleeting moment, as the words vibrated, tangible in the air, Titus Cariad felt a glimmer of belief. He felt a twinge of optimism rise, delicately unfurling like a rainbow of brightness. Despite his current blockage, he clung to that phrase, allowing it to kindle a spark within him, to ignite a fiery fervency. The path might now be unclear, the way may obscured, the visions might be elusive, there may be a sinister evil lurking, but one thing was certain, the message was loud and clear.

Find Jess.

The spirits had spoken. Jess's fate was his to uncover, and he would do whatever he could to bring her back, out of the shadows that concealed her.

Determined to unravel the mystery that shrouded Jessie's strange disappearance, The Visionary, Titus Cariad, made a decision. With a furrowed brow and a renewed sense of purpose, he began his descent from his lofty woodland outcrop in the mountains. With Ryoni at his heels, he travelled down into the valley.

Each step he took carried him closer to the quaint area he was tasked to guide, the area known as Hallowed Brook, the place where Troy, Blue, and Ky made their home.

Despite his age, his towering stature granted him a commanding presence, and each step that he took was powerful, filled with fervour, bringing him closer to the answers he sought.

The loyal Shadow Wolf, bounded at his side, their

strides in harmony with the rhythm of Celestia itself. With the eternal beat of the planet's heart. It's soul. The journey, while slowed by uneven terrain and lush, overgrown landscapes, posed no great challenge to Titus' giant form. He moved with a steady grace that belied his age, each thundering step carried him closer to the heart of his destination. His stary robes dancing around him.

The wind whispered through the trees, a soft symphony that followed his journey like a troubadour's melody. As the scent of the earth mingled with the fragrance of wildflowers, Titus's thoughts were clear except for his one repeating desire. He wanted to seek answers, to unravel the truth of Jess's disappearance, and to offer his guidance in any way he could. Sparked by Troy's visit, he knew now that this was the way forward.

During his journey, The Visionary, looked skyward, his gaze drawn toward the vast expanse above. There, against the canvas of Celestia's ever-changing skies, a magnificent sight buoyed him. The Devout Drolle, that majestic creature of the heavens, graced the thermals with its captivating presence. Swooping down from the ice-capped peaks.

Its sapphire-hued feathers shimmered like gemstones beneath the sun's gilded caress, each hue merging and shifting as it effortlessly rode the currents. A beak of radiant gold caught the light, a beacon of splendour that contrasted with the boundless blue around it. With elegant poise and effortless grace, the Devout Drolle glided through the sky, a symbol of the harmonious dance between all living creatures and the elements. He knew his calling now. He must protect them all.

As Titus Cariad watched this awe-inspiring spectacle, a hushed reverence settled upon him. The Devout Drolle was no ordinary being; it was a creature touched by the spirits, an embodiment of the higher realm's presence within the flora and fauna of Celestia.

He took this wondrous sight as another message, another whispered through the winds, delivered by the spirits that guided his visions. The Devout Drolle's presence cemented the importance of his quest, lending weight to his thirst for answers, and fuelling his drive to uncover the truths hidden within the shadows. The spirits wishes were strong.

Gratitude swelled in his heart, his faith felt restored, and the elements praised him. Titus Cariad continued his journey down towards Hallowed Brook. The image of the Devout Drolle remained imprinted in his mind, a symbol of the unity between the realms, and a sign of the power of connection, the connections that would guide him on the right path to Jessie.

With his giant strides, the journey that might have taken others an hour or two, passed in mere moments. The mountains seemed to bow before his very presence, the valleys acknowledging his divinity.

As Hallowed Brook came into view, Titus' heart stirred, driven by strength and hope.

He carried with him an artefact, a token of trade that would serve as a ruse to initiate conversation. First with Ky, and then the others. He understood the delicate nature of what he set out to achieve, was wary of the need to tread lightly as he navigated the twisted tunnels of secrets and the deep caves of curious occurrences.

Stepping into Hallowed Brook, Titus' towering form cast a long shadow over the familiar landscape. Ryoni, his wolf was a symbol of loyal support. Of the complex connection between man and beast.

As he approached Ky's trading post, a sense of quiet authority enveloped him. His age had gifted him wisdom, his stature, an imposing presence that commanded respect, his worldliness, the art of subtle persuasion.

And so, with the echoes of Celestia's winds and whispers as his guide, Titus Cariad entered the centre of Hallowed Brook, ready to listen to their tales, ready to ask probing questions. But, most importantly, he wanted to uncover the truths that would illuminate the way to Jess. To discover exactly where she could be found.

The spirits had spoken.

CHAPTER 13

BLUE

Cocooned within the comforting walls of her treehouse home, stroking Scruffy, her cat, in an attempt to soothe her mind, Blue's thoughts still continued to churn. Her stomach writhed with tumbling, twisting worry. The weight of Jessie's absence continually bore down heavily upon her shoulders, adding to her pain; the concern for her friend's safety gnawed at her. She couldn't rest. She couldn't switch off. As her mind spiralled and span with thoughts of potential clues and areas to search, she also fretted about the fact that Troy's priorities lay elsewhere. He was focused on providing food to the Capital Core. He was under pressure and wouldn't want them to take a break from The Elysium Fields. She knew in her heart that he'd react badly to Ky's idea of a quest to the lake. Blue and Ky were his strongest workers. Even with Blue struggling with her back.

But a deeper anxiety grew within her. A jittery, nauseous fear that her persistent back problems might slow down any efforts to search within the Desire Mountain range. She knew that her pain, the stiffness, was particularly disabling at the moment. Her neck and back felt like stone. She'd tried to hide it, but the truth was unavoidable. Blue nibbled at her fingers as she worried that she would hinder their progress. A sigh escaped her lips; she would be floored by guilt if that were to happen.

Buried by what ifs.

As she wrestled with the bleakness in her head, the world around her seemed to shift. The ground trembled. A rumbling, thudding vibration that caused her to jump up with a start. At first, Blue wondered if there was a powerful storm coming.

Thundering thuds resonated through the air, coupled with the rustling of leaves and the swaying of branches. The sudden flight of countless birds startled Blue. Their fretful calls rose to the heavens, their wings flapping in fright. Blue's gaze was drawn beyond her window, her eyes widening as she spotted a sight that she had never imagined seeing here in the middle of the Brook.

Through the parting trees, out of the whispering foliage, a huge figure emerged. A giant. His colossal presence reached up to the highest boughs. In the company of a Shadow Wolf, the giant bounded through the landscape with a grace that belied his enormous stature. It was The Visionary, Titus Cariad himself. Blue inched closer to the window, fascinated.

Confusion and surprise rose within Blue, as she watched the giant stomp down, getting closer to the treehouses and the small village centre. A tinge of disbelief made her squint her eyes and wrinkle up her nose. What was he doing here? The Visionary was a figure rarely seen beyond his mountainous realm. She knew that Titus was a being of wisdom and foresight, a seer who lived above the valley. He spent his time apart from the inhabitants of Hallowed Brook, communing with the spirits. If you wanted to see The Visionary, you went to him. You asked for an audience. He didn't come down to you. His potions and spells were the stuff of legends, tales from the elders. Yet here he was, carrying a cloth bag and striding with purpose, headed to the heart of their settlement.

As The Visionary's footsteps carried him closer, Blue's shock and surprise became intrigue. What could this mean? What was the purpose of his unexpected visit? Could he have news? Questions tumbled like falling shovels full of dirt, muddying her mind, and, at the same time, a flicker of a small fragile flame began to spark within her. A dim hope. Perhaps he held answers, insight, or guidance that could lead them to Jess.

Blue wasn't a strong believer in the spirits, Jess always had been though. She was fascinated by the other realm. Could this be the beginnings of a breakthrough?

With her heart in her mouth, her pulse racing and a desperate urge to clutch onto any fragment of hope, Blue prepared to face The Visionary. The giant's presence caused a mixture of longing and dread to course through her veins. For a second, she felt frozen.

From her vantage point within the tall treehouse, Blue's gaze remained fixed on the unfolding scene before her. The giant form of The Visionary approached Ky's modest trading shed. This structure that had always been dwarfed by its surroundings, now appeared even more fragile and ramshackle in comparison to the giant's hulking frame. Curiosity gripped Blue as she watched the unlikely meeting. Scruffy, her black and white cat, wove his lithe body in front of her face, arching his back and flicking his tail, the fur-ball partially obscuring her view.

"Scruffy, no. Get down from there," Blue whispered impatiently.

With a tiny gasp, Blue's eyes widened as Ky emerged from his trading shed, his usually animated, jokiness replaced by a hushed awe. She watched as his chin almost hit the floor before he peered up at the towering figure before him.

As the giant extended a greeting, before reaching into the bag he carried, Blue felt her heart skip a beat. Her gaze was fixed on the object that emerged, an object that she had seen before. She gripped the window ledge. Blue's breath caught in her throat as recognition dawned, like a flame igniting then flaring within the folds of her memories.

A golden sundial. A relic that she had seen depicted using coloured pencils, sketched, within one of Jessie's scrapbooks. A way marker that had been immortalised upon the pages of her friend's colourful diaries. This must be something that Jess had seen on one of her journeys. Blue was sure of it.

When she had first seen it, the sundial's image had seared into her mind for its sheer beauty. And, in the afternoon light, it glowed just as Jess had drawn it within her books. Exactly the same enchanting preciousness.

She scrambled across the room, reaching to grasp Jessie's sketchbook, the one that lay in the corner, still in its cloth bag. When she had it, she raced back to the window, her stomach flipping and her legs feeling weak.

As she watched The Visionary present the golden sundial to Ky, Blue's mind tried to untangle the knots. What did this mean? Why had he brought this particular artefact? Did it hold any significance to the disappearance of her best friend?

Blue's thoughts whirled around her head, her hands slowly finding the page that held the drawing of the sundial. They trembled and she willed them to steady. She stared at it open mouthed, seeing the words that were delicately written nearby.

> *I turn to the one*
> *Who sees*
> *Trying to seek*
> *Peace.*

She had visited him. The Visionary, Jess had been to Titus Cariad. She had sketched his hut. With a sense of energy, a buoyancy that quickened her pulse even further, Blue realised that this realisation could hold significance beyond words. He might have answers. The giant's visit, the golden sundial, it was all linked to Jess. She knew it. She felt it in her stiff bones.

As Ky accepted the glowing treasure, Blue was sure that this was a step. A step towards the moment when the curious pieces of this confusing puzzle would finally slot together. Then they would reveal truths that had remained hidden. Hidden and buried within the murky, shadowy lands of Celestia.

CHAPTER 14

TROY

"Titus?"

Troy's heart hammered within his chest as he trudged back from Elysium Fields, catching sight of The Visionary thundering through the Brook. He stopped dumbfounded. Titus Cariad was standing large as life by Ky's trading post. The gasped words escaped his mouth before he had a chance to register the thought. A mixture of shock, surprise and suspicion gripped him, his mind raced to figure out the implications of this unexpected visitor. Why was Titus here so soon after Troy had been to seek his guidance? Would he reveal The Calete family secrets? What would Blue think?

His family's murky dealings flashed before his eyes, like dirty shadows lurking in the shady corners of his inner consciousness.

For a moment, he hesitated, his feet rooted to the ground as his thoughts spiralled.

What if The Visionary had come to seek retribution? What if his own past, his family's secrets, were exposed to everyone? What would his aunt do then? Troy gulped feeling the hairs on the back of his neck stand to attention. His aunt, Eliza Calete's, stern face loomed in his mind, her red hair like a fire of fury. Her formidable features were an embodiment of the harsh authority and obsession with power that had shaped his upbringing. Try as he might, he hadn't been able to escape it. His father was a genuine, hardworking man, but Terrence's sister Eliza was the complete opposite. They were like light and dark. Eliza held the strings of power, the strings of control as well as the strings of all of their financial affairs. And the strings were grimy, he didn't want to be tangled in them anymore.

As the moments ticked by, a decision flashed in Troy's mind. Perhaps it was a cowardly move, but he decided that, for now, he would avoid The Visionary. He'd steer clear of any conversations that could reveal more than he was willing to face right now. He had said far too much already. As he stared across the fields, Troy felt like he was falling down a deep hole. His instincts clamoured for him to seek protection, to safeguard the reputation of his family. Troy knew it was wrong, that he should face the darkness, but the burden tied up in his name, was a powerful force.

Unsure of whether this was the right thing to do, wracked with doubt, he turned away from the Brook regardless. Cursing his fear of his aunt.

Troy slipped back into his treehouse to check on the injured animal, the little Lunafi. Relief flooded him as he saw the creature's peaceful slumber, his brain briefly distracted from the chaos of his dark thoughts. At least Luna was on the mend.

"Rest well," he murmured softly, a glimmer of tears shining in his eyes. The gentle, furry creature made him feel a rush of love; he hated how the Brook was changing. The Lunafi's silvery, purple fur shimmered in the light, it seemed like a precious statue. He took one final look, then climbed down the treehouse rungs.

Troy's purposeful strides carried him out of the Brook and toward the ancestral Calete home. He approached the large treehouse, perched beside the babbling water, marvelling at its ornate beauty. How could something so magnificent be connected to so much dirt? His gaze lingered on the unnaturally green waters; he gritted his teeth. The house stood as a silent witness to generations and generations of suspicious history, shady secrets and shadowy lies. It stung.

As he got closer, meandering down the sweeping drive, staring up at the polished wood, his earlier confidence became perilously thin. He gulped as he trudged down the twisting path, stepping over puddles, avoiding places where the mud grasped at his feet, pulling him downwards. Troy tried hard not to slip in the squelching dirt.

He entered the large expanse of garden with a mixture of steely determination and shaking panic. The air bristled, explosive with tension.

Eliza Calete's sharp gaze met his as soon as he began to climb the sturdy wooden steps, the wide staircase that wound upwards to the home of his childhood. Eliza's sharp, angular face betrayed her true feelings. She couldn't hide her displeasure.

"Troy," her voice was as crisp as the sun withered vegetables they collected, her tone edged with sharp curiosity. Eliza's flame-red hair coiled around her pale face.

"So, to what do I owe the pleasure of your presence nephew? Problems in the fields? Has something happened with the forage?"

Troy swallowed, his hooded eyes meeting hers with growing unease.

"No, this is something else." Eliza's green eyes flashed with something indistinct.

"Aunt Eliza," he began, his voice threaded with formality. "I thought it was time we had a conversation. About the dirt. About the past.

About your plans."

Eliza's gaze remained fixed upon him, her expression, as usual, worryingly unreadable.

"Spit it out boy, stop teetering around the cliff edge? What do you mean... the past? My plans? Be clear," her tone was caustic, the weight of their shared history writhing, twisting deep beneath the surface.

Troy took a deep breath, steadying himself. Her eyes bore into him. Those emerald-green eyes that lacked an ounce of warmth. They were like cold gemstones, changed by time and pressure. Formed after many years in stone.

"I mean the things that are affecting the Brook. The secrets you've already buried. And yes," he continued as her eyes widened; his words were direct. "There are things...things that you should know that I know."

A flicker of surprise crossed Eliza's features before being swiftly masked. Hidden away.

"And what prompted this sudden urge for disclosure nephew dear? Why now? You want to come clean? You're willing to risk it all?"

Troy felt his heart pierce with her sharp accusation. Still, he wouldn't be deterred.

"A friend. A friend and the truth, Aunt Eliza. It's time we faced it, together. I know they're linked."

The silence that followed was heavy, a palpable thick cloud of mistrust, a fog that seemed to engulf them.

As Eliza's gaze skewered him, Troy braced himself for the bitter unearthing that surely lay ahead. An unearthing of revelations, of hazards. The necessary reveal of a past that had remained concealed, buried in the dirty ground for far too long.

Troy's words cut through the fog, a note of urgency evident as he confronted his aunt, his voice laced with grit. "Aunt Eliza, The Visionary is here, he's come down from the mountains to visit Hallowed Brook. He's digging around."

Eliza Calete stepped back, her boots clattering on the wooden floor. Despite her shock, her face remained stoic. To Troy, her expression was a mask. A mask of composure. She took seconds to absorb the news.

"The Visionary," she repeated dryly, her tone tinkling with an iron harshness.

Troy's chestnut eyes met hers, a mixture of suspicion and determination evident in his gaze.

"Eliza, I can't shake this bad feeling I have about his presence. It's as if he knows something, something that could unravel our secrets. All of them. Could the spirits have revealed something?"

He stared at her then as his lies were caught up in the dirt laced words. He could play the game too. She'd taught him well.

The ticking clock, behind her in the grand treehouse, seemed to still, to hold its breath, a palpable tension filling the air as Troy dug in further.

"And there's something else," he continued, his voice firm. "I know you're keeping something from me, something about Jess. Perhaps he knows?"

Eliza's gaze met his, her eyes like obscured windows. Sealed and shuttered windows that hid the deeper truth. The truth that she had long kept hidden. A shadow of something unreadable flitted across her features, her lips forming a grim thin line.

Troy's determination only grew stronger, he sensed weakness. His longing for answers, his feelings for Blue and his intuition about what lay beneath the surface spurred him on.

"Jess is my friend, aunt Eliza. I deserve to know the full story, what has happened to her. Her friends... well... we're all going out of our minds."

The room felt charged with unspoken accusations, a heavy silence punctuated by the bleakness of their shared history was like a bomb stilled in mid-air. A bomb that would explode eventually.

Eliza's gaze held Troy's, a battle of hidden motives and long-held secrets raging between them.

After a moment, Eliza's expression shifted, her features tightening with firmness, became even harder. Her voice, when it finally emerged, held an edge of steely grittiness.

"Troy, nephew. There are things you are better off not knowing. Some secrets are meant to be buried. To always stay in the dirt."

Troy's heart raced, the gravity of their conversation sinking in. He met Eliza's gaze with a mixture of fear and desperation. His voice rose a notch as he pressed his aunt, letting her know he wasn't just going to let her dig her heels in. He wanted to make crystal clear the fact that he would not stop sifting until he found exactly what he was looking for. Despite her trying to block his way.

"But Jess is my friend Eliza. I need to know what has happened to her. Where she is."

Eliza's eyes pierced his, a chilling glint betraying the depths of her malice. "Some paths lead to darkness, Troy," she replied, her voice a chilling whisper. The threat like a blaring alarm. "Some might drive you underground, to bury you. I believe that It's best if you remain on the path you're on."

"But…what about my father?"

"Terrence is sick Troy, very sick. You'd do well to remember his frailty. In all honesty nephew, you'd do well to remember your place too. People can get lost when they forget their place."

Troy's breath caught and he took a step backwards. She smiled then, an evil smirk that told Troy she had him snared.

As the full weight of Eliza's malevolence became clear to him, he realised the depths of her determination to protect the family secrets, to shield their dirt from the light of day. As he faced her unwavering tenacity, he knew that he was embarking on a journey. A journey with obstacles: stubborn lies, secrets, and a stand-off that had been a long time coming.

He needed to be prepared.

"I'll head back to work," Troy muttered.

CHAPTER 15

JESS

Within the confines of her rocky cave, her bleak cell for the last few months, Jessie's emotions were a hurricane, a whirlwind of dreams, despair, and determination. Her heart clung to the fragments of memories that she had captured within her sketchbooks back in Hallowed Brook. The sketches, feathers, shells and snippets of poetry that were the record of her journeys.

Here she had tried to recreate some of those same memories, etching them painstakingly onto the stone. Each wall filled with the very essence of her. With her life, her love.

Each stroke of her hand on the cave's surface felt like a connection to a world beyond her confinement. The world of freedom, creativity, and the cherished bonds with nature that had once defined her life.

But her thoughts were shattered by the intrusion of a new presence. One of the eerie, faceless Droids that seemed to just materialise within her cave. Panic welled within her chest as she watched its red laser eye sweep across the space, her mind blank with fear. Were they here to end her, to silence her for good?

As the Droids held her by the shoulders, her heart fluttered rapidly inside her chest, and the dread and uncertainty threatened to bury her. The shadowy darkness of her surroundings seemed to engulf her, pulling her down further into the gloom.

"I'm sorry for the intrusion," one of the Droids spoke, its voice surprisingly respectful. "We've been instructed to relocate you to another cave. Please let us escort you."

Jess had little option.

She wasn't moved far, this was a larger space, drier. The constant drip absent, like her sketches, her words. Her breath caught as the Droids noticed her torn dress, she was sure they'd realise what she had done. But she watched with surprise and confusion as they presented her with a new one. She warily took in the all-black loose smock, the fabric felt foreign against her skin. She quickly changed into it, covering her modesty by holding up her old dress in front of her. The drab, shapelessness felt like a stark contrast to the vibrant colours of her usual clothes.

Observing her unease, another Droid spoke softly, its tone carrying a hint of understanding which jarred her. They were machines.

"We noticed your dress was torn. We hope this replacement is suitable."

The changed clothing was simultaneously a gesture of care and a stark reminder of her captivity. She realised she looked just like them. All black, all the same.

The Droids seemed to tread incredibly carefully around her, a change from before. Their words and actions were now a display of respect and duty. Something had changed. Something fundamental. Something puzzling. Were these the same Droids that had thrown her food tray on the floor? Jess couldn't be sure.

As she took in these new surroundings, Jess became aware of the absence of loose stones, of anything she could use to create pictures on the rock. She realised she would be unable to scratch the drawings into the rock face as she has done in her previous cave. The emptiness was a reminder of the control the Droids exerted over her. This space, although more comfortable was both a cage and a symbol of her isolation.

The rough iron bed and thin mattress should have provided some relief, a small respite from the hardships she had endured. The other cell's cold jagged floor and continual puddles that had added to her daily misery. And yet, amidst the cell's small luxuries, a sense of foreboding settled over her. Jess couldn't shake the feeling that these small comforts could be a way to lull her, a sense of security, her guard lowered, before she faced something much more ominous.

As the hours stretched into night, Jess grappled with stomach sinking fears. The bed, the dress, the food, the clean water, the lack of chains and tethers. It all felt like a trick. An evil prank.

The hope she had once held onto with shaking fingers began to unravel slowly but surely in her mind. Jess was facing the unnerving possibility of death here. Death because of what she had uncovered. Because of her delving. Would she be left to rot here? To mix in with the soil, to become the dirt.

CHAPTER 16

THE VISIONARY

On his descent from his woodland outcrop, Titus Cariad's steps were steady, each step bringing him lower, echoing through the whole area, the echoes seemed like a drumbeat, a war cry, a reminder of his need to fight for the truth.

The journey, effortless for a giant of his stature, allowed him to reach Hallowed Brook in next to no time. Ryoni, his faithful Shadow Wolf, trotted alongside him. His fur glistening in the light. Titus appreciated the company.

As he approached Ky's dilapidated trading shed, the building seemed almost comically small in comparison to his massive frame. Titus paused at the entrance, lowering himself with care to avoid causing any damage to the shack. He peered within.

Ky quickly emerged, his eyes widening as he took in the sight of the towering Visionary and the large Shadow Wolf. For a second, he stood silent, gazing upwards, his mouth agape.

With a small gesture that could have passed as a smile, Titus extended the bag he carried towards Ky.

"I've brought you something, something to trade," he said, he kept his voice soft despite his size, like the whispering of the breeze through the trees. Titus watched

Ky closely.

The man's gaze flickered from the bag to Titus, curiosity evident in his expression. His eyes were filled with confusion.

"Visionary, well this is a surprise. What's in the bag?"

Titus inclined his head.

"It's an item that means a lot to me, I've heard about others appreciation for your work, for the care you take with precious treasures. Your reputation goes before you. So, I brought you a relic of times past. To see what you can get for it."

Titus watched as Ky cautiously accepted the bag, he glanced inside and then back up at Titus, a mixture of surprise and shock upon his furrowed brow. His face seemed momentarily startled, like he had seen something in the folds of his brain, a memory, a nugget he had secreted away.

"A golden sundial? This is quite something Titus. Where is it from?"

The Visionary's lilac eyes met Ky's, he tried to sound sincere.

"You have an eye for antiquities. I thought you might appreciate it. It's a magical thing, someone will surely want to trade for it. I think it should fetch a handsome price. Will you try?"

Ky's curiosity seemed to deepen as he studied the sundial in his hand. Titus noticed the precious gold gleaming in the light.

"This has a special history behind it, doesn't it? What's the story?"

Titus felt a wave of nostalgia as he replied,

"It's a relic of a time long gone, a gift from the spirits from my early days. A reminder of the paths we have to walk, and the moments left to cherish. I keep it by my hut, to tell the time. But now, it's time for it to pass to someone else. The time has come for me to recognise the fading of the light. My days in this realm are short."

Ky's attention shifted, a thoughtful expression settling over him. Titus could see the cogs whirring in his head and realised that this man was as sharp as a blade.

"Speaking of paths and moments, Titus, I can't help but feel that you've come down from your hut up there for more than just this."

Titus nodded; he was right about this man. The corners of his huge mouth twitched into a grin at Ky's directness. Sharp and straight to the point, this one was not easily deceived.

"Indeed, Ky. I've come with questions."

Ky's brows lifted; his curiosity clearly aroused. "Questions? About what?"

"About your friend, Jessie, the one who's gone missing. I am worried that Jessie's disappearance has a deeper significance for the future of Celestia," Titus answered, his tone far more serious.

Ky glanced up at the giant in astonishment. Titus saw the pain in his eyes.

"Jess? You know about her...Yes, she vanished...just gone. We are getting more and more concerned each day that she's been missing. It's just not normal. Have you discovered something Visionary? What do you need to know?"

Titus's eyes held a mixture of knowledge and

frustration.

"I've reached out to the spirits, but their guidance has been elusive. I have theories, but nothing absolute."

Ky's face turned grim.

"You suspect she's in trouble then, like we do?"

Titus nodded. This Ky was indeed bright.

"I fear so yes. I know that you're close to her. That she's a friend. So, I'm here to ask you about what you know."

Titus watched his expressions closely. Ky's lips formed a thoughtful line as he considered the question.

"Jess kept scrapbooks... she has a passion for exploring, for sketching, for writing. She's left a trail of her journeys within those pages. Blue brought one to me... there was a map."

Titus felt his mind sharpen with interest. He leaned in closer.

"A map, hidden within her scrapbooks?"

"Yes, Blue is determined to find her. She's not one to back down from a challenge, and she believes this map... well...that it holds clues to her whereabouts."

Titus hunched down slightly; his lilac eyes locked onto Ky's. His meaty thighs bent. "Clues that could lead you to her?"

"That's the hope, at least. Blue believes that Jess may have been captured, and the map could be the key to finding her," Ky added, his expression serious as he looked into the giant's eyes.

Titus sighed; his fingers absentmindedly traced the Visitotem that he carried at his side.

"I'll need to speak with Blue as well, learn more about

the map, the scrapbooks, and her memories of the last days that Jess was here in Hallowed Brook."

"Troy's involved too, you know. Troy Calete. He's our friend and our boss," Ky's tone rang with a hint of worry, a distinct flicker of concern was evident in his eyes.

"Noted."

Their conversation continued, the weight of Jessie's disappearance underpinning their words. As they spoke of scrapbooks, sketches, and hidden maps, Titus Cariad's mind turned over all possibilities, his connection to the spirits guiding his intuition. Ryoni stirred by his side as if tracking something in the trees. The wolf's guard was up, its ears were flat, and his body poised to lunge. There was a restless whine. Titus shivered.

Ky's voice held a hint of excitement as he shared his plans. "You know, Blue and I were planning to head up to Lumina Lake. It's a trek I know, but it's on the map and in the scrapbooks, we thought it might be a place where we could spot something."

As he spoke, the serene atmosphere was suddenly broken by the appearance of a magnificent figure soaring overhead. The Devout Drolle's sapphire feathers glinted in the sunlight, its wings beating rhythmically as it rode the thermals with agility and grace. Both Ky and Titus gazed in awe; their discussion momentarily forgotten.

Ryoni, the loyal Shadow Wolf, barked with urgency. His ears were now pricked forward, and his gaze seemed fixed on the majestic bird above. He whimpered.

"That's not an ordinary reaction," Titus mused, "He's trying to tell us something."

The Visionary's enormous, lilac eyes narrowed as he

watched Ryoni closely, his eyes moving from the wolf then up to the sky.

"Animals have a way of sensing things beyond our perception. Perhaps Ryoni senses a connection, a message." The ancient giant murmured the words, almost to himself.

As if in response, the Devout Drolle let out a resounding call that pierced the damp air, a melodic blend of notes that seemed to vibrate with an otherworldly energy. Ryoni immediately gave a low, almost reverent howl that resonated with the song of the majestic bird.

Ky's brows furrowed as he looked between the two creatures, an idea seemed to be forming in his mind. "What if... what if Ryoni and the Devout Drolle are connected somehow? They're both responding to the call, as if they share a bond. Is that possible Visionary?"

Titus considered it. "Perhaps, these connections do happen. It may be a bond that could hold significance for us. Perhaps the spirits are trying to communicate through them."

He thought about how his visions had felt blocked. How something was in the way. How he had felt frustrated. Could the spirits be trying another way?

Ryoni's strange baying and the Devout Drolle's call seemed to blend together, creating a harmonious duet that electrified the surroundings. The wind carried their voices, a magical symphony of nature that stirred the air around them. The whole of Hallowed Brook seemed alive with sound and movement. People had come down from their treehouses to stare. The muddy fields were crowded with Celestians. When they noticed him, the giant in their midst, their amazement only grew.

"It could be that the Devout Drolle is trying to lead us somewhere, sending a message."

Ky's gaze shifted then from the soaring Devout Drolle to Titus, his excitement evident, the possibilities flashing in his eyes.

"You know, I think Blue and I need to explore Lumina Lake as soon as possible. Next to the lake, in her scrapbook, Jessie sketched the Devout Drolle soaring high."

Titus Cariad paused. His lilac eyes seemed to hold a mixture of caution, consideration and care.

"Exploration can reveal both wonders and dangers. But if you truly believe that Lumina Lake holds answers, then it's worth a trek up there."

Ky's enthusiasm rang around the clearing.

"I think it's something we have to do Titus. We just need to be prepared, take it steady, since Blue's been struggling with her back. And of course, we'll need to get Troy's permission, seeing as he's our boss."

Titus nodded in agreement, his voice carrying a hint of wisdom.

"It is always considered wise to approach such journeys with watchfulness. Be alert. The Desire Mountains can be a realm of both beauty and mystery."

Ky looked up at The Visionary's towering frame, staring into his eyes with a questioning intensity.

"What do you think Titus? Do you sense anything about this journey? Is there something that you've seen?"

The giant's expression turned thoughtful; he spoke with truth.

"I sense curiosity and determination within you Ky.

Just remember, while Lumina Lake may hold answers, it's wise to tread with caution. Curious things often lurk within the Desire Mountains."

"Curious things? Like what?"

The Visionary looked upwards; his words laced with mystery.

"Creatures that defy imagination, secrets that have been hidden for years. The mountains have their own way of testing those who seek their truths."

"Understood Titus. We'll be careful."

"Good. Remember, the journey itself can often be as enlightening as the destination. And with the Devout Drolle's presence guiding you, you may find that the path reveals more than you expect." Even to Titus Cariad, his words sounded like a riddle.

As Ky was mulling over the peculiar words, the majestic bird continued to ride the currents above them. It seemed like a symbol, a sign of the mysteries that lay in the upper reaches of The Desire Mountains.

Ryoni seemed to sense something in the trees again, his hackles were raised and his focus narrowed to something up in the canopy. Titus Cariad thought he saw a brief flash of red.

When he looked again, it had gone.

CHAPTER 17

BLUE

B lue watched as Ky gestured towards her treehouse, their conversation clearly turning in her direction. It was bound to.

Hopefulness continued to swell deep within her. She had heard many tales of the giant who resided in the mountains, she knew all about the wise man with visions, but she had never actually chosen to seek his guidance for herself. The idea of spirits and visions felt a little foreign to her, the other realm too ethereal, yet the desperation to find Jess overrode her scepticism. For now, at least. Ky, spotting her watching, gestured for her to join them.

Ky had led Titus Cariad away from the growing bustle of activity outside his trading post, guiding him to the tranquil expanse of the Hallowed Brook meeting room. Here, in a large shelter, amidst the towering trees and the babble of the brook, they could find some privacy. The spacious gathering space offered enough room for the giant to sit comfortably, his large body filling a snug area towards the back. Away from the prying eyes of curious onlookers, perhaps they could talk without being heard. Maybe Blue could share her side of the story.

Trepidation gnawed at Blue as she approached the gathering space at the far reaches of Hallowed Brook, her heart fluttering like a Halcyon butterfly in her chest. Like the purple, gossamer winged butterfly that lived in the trees by her home. She couldn't seem to ignore the fact that Jessie's disappearance had plunged her into a world of wariness. Bewilderment made her feel dizzy, trusting no one and doubting everything. So, if Titus Cariad held any answers, she needed to hear them, she needed to get some peace.

Ryoni, the Shadow Wolf, greeted her with a suspicious sniff as she entered, making her stomach sink. Others around them gawked and whispered, pointing at the lofty giant with his shiny head and magic staff, but Ky expertly shooed them away, allowing her a moment of privacy with Titus.

With the hulking presence of The Visionary before her, his lilac eyes exuding a stoic air of wisdom, Blue found her throat constricted, the need to tell all making her tremble. Her words choked her and her chest ached with the loss she needed to reveal.

"Titus, I... I'm Blue," she began, her reedy voice betraying her nervousness. "Ky came to me, he said you might have insights about Jessie's disappearance."

Titus Cariad's direct, lilac eyes met hers, piercing into her very soul, the expression on his ancient, brown face was both inquisitive and probing. The lines of many years, like the ancient map, traversed his features.

"Indeed Blue, welcome. I am uneasy about Jess, I feel a sense of worry for her," he replied, his deep voice resonating with power. "The spirits guide me in mysterious ways, I've tried to seek their direction, their divine support regarding Jess. I can't see exactly where she is, but I feel she is alive and what she knows is important to the whole of Celestia. She carries a secret."

Blue's chest was tight, her eyes unconsciously welling with tears, her nervousness began to melt away as she sensed Titus Cariad's genuine desire to help them, to help her find Jess. Her relief at the word alive was palpable, it buoyed her. Blue's hesitancy disappeared like Jess herself. All of a sudden, she found herself opening up, sharing her memories of Jessie's last days. She recalled her best friend's jittery nervous energy, and the cryptic warning she had given Blue about Troy and his family.

"Her voice was cold, and she looked...scared...scared for me somehow. She was rarely scared. Ever."

"And you say that she mentioned Troy Calete directly?" Titus asked.

Nodding, she explained what she had seen in Jessie's sketch books, the drawings, the map concealed in the back, she flushed as she withheld certain information from the imposing giant. The sketches of the eerie black figures with red slits for eyes, as well as her suspicion that Jess had been to visit Titus too.

"There's a lot of sketches that I don't properly understand, they don't seem to have any meaning," she said. It felt odd, but she had a growing fear that those black figures with the red eyes could jeopardise Jessie's safety. Her gut roiled, silencing her words.

The conversation began to turn as Titus probed deeper. He asked further questions about Jessie's warnings, wanting to know more about her friend's worry, why she had seemed troubled by Blue's relationship with Troy. But Blue didn't know. She didn't know then and she didn't know now either.

Her heart sank as footsteps echoed behind her and Troy strode into the gathering space. He looked wide eyed and confused, his face falling as he took in their unexpected visitor. Blue knew him well, he didn't like feeling out of control, like he wasn't in charge. They'd blindsided him. He'd been raised to lead, to be the boss. She winced as she realised how this looked, like they were being disloyal, talking out of turn.

"What's all this about me?" his voice cut through the air like a sharpened blade. His gaze shifted from Blue to Ky, then back to her, flitting like a captured song bird, suspicion was clear in his wounded expression. Something hard too.

Caught off guard, Blue shot a hesitant glance at Ky. Her legs became weak. She could sense the tension in the air, the weight pushing her down, her back screeching. Taking a deep breath. Blue's heart pounded as she tried to find the right words, words that wouldn't wound him like she had the other day. She didn't want to hurt him, she just wanted answers.

As she struggled to speak, Titus Cariad's large form, his hands outstretched in a placating gesture, brought a sense of serenity to the highly charged atmosphere that sizzled between them, his soft words resonating like a reassuring melody. His years of guidance rang like a familiar tune.

"Troy, welcome. We are here for answers. To try to locate your friend. I can understand the emotional turmoil that this may be causing you, the mentions of your family, the business, but the aim here remains unchanged. We all want to bring Jess back to the Brook."

Blue watched as Troy's tense stature changed, he gradually became more pliant. Like them all, he fell under the hypnotic spell of the giant's calming presence.

Ky's voice echoed The Visionary's words.

"Hey, c'mon, it's not just about you. I swear. No way buddy. Look we were discussing Jess, that's all Troy. Desperately trying to piece together what exactly has happened to her. We've got to try and find out. It's been too long."

Troy's eyes narrowed; he bristled. Blue saw his posture become defensive again and his chestnut eyes bored into his best friend; like he was challenging him to a duel.

"Okay Ky, you want to play hero, I get it. But why do I feel like there's more to this than you're letting on?"

Blue's heart skipped a beat as the seconds slowly ticked by, uncertainty and apprehension swirling around her again. In that charged moment, she realised that their journey to uncover the truth had taken an unexpected turn; one that might harm their friendship forever.

What was he hiding?

She gulped, wide-eyed, as everything seemed to hang in the balance, as her whole world seemed to be crumbling once more. Blue felt like she was sinking in murky, soggy ground. The black hole of depression sucked her downwards, claiming her.

Blue and Ky exchanged a worried glance, their words momentarily frozen. Her mind raced, they were friends, more than friends. She didn't want this awkwardness to spoil what they had, but she couldn't help but feel he knew something, something about why Jessie may be missing.

Ky's voice remained calm, as he attempted to defuse the situation.

"Boss... hey, look Troy, Titus here has an inkling about Jessie, that what's happened is important... bigger than just our friend not coming back. He thinks there is something more insisted behind it all and he wanted to know some things, so we were just discussing the strange circumstances around Jess's disappearance. You know how much she means to us. How much she means to us all."

Troy's brow furrowed, his eyes narrowing. He was hopping mad with them behind his grim stare; Blue could sense it.

"I get it, I do. It's just... unsettling to have people speculating about... well about me and my family. About the past... our business."

The giant's response was soothing once more, his age and experience obvious, "I understand," he said, his voice even. "But rest assured, I'm here to ask questions, not to suggest that anyone is to blame. We're all united in our quest for answers. We're here to uncover the truth behind Jess's disappearance. She means a lot to many; my one desire is to ensure her safe return. I'm sure you want that too..."

Blue sensed a shift in Troy's demeanour, a gradual release of tension as Titus' words sank in.

"Yes, of course that's what I want. Perhaps you're right. I shouldn't let my selfish emotions cloud the truth, it's a fact that she's gone, it's time to admit that we all believe that Jessie has vanished... and that she's vanished suspiciously."

"Exactly," Titus replied, "By sharing what we know

and looking for further clues, for signs, then we may have a chance of solving this mystery, of finding Jessie. Of bringing her back to you all."

Standing beside Troy, so close she could almost ouch him, Blue felt a warmth radiating in her chest, she dared to dream, to hope that Jess could be found. That they would find her together. Blue's gaze met Troy's, a swirl of emotions dancing in her eyes. She saw the familiarity, the connection they had built over time, and she hoped they could find their way through this. But, most importantly, she needed her friend back by her side. It consumed her.

Her gaze dipped briefly, her voice softening. "You know I care about her, about finding her. It's all I can think about. But there's... something more, Troy. Something Jess mentioned about your family, their connections, the darkness she felt... she was trying to warn me of something..." Blue's words were carefully chosen, each syllable felt explosive, heavy, weighed down with the gravity of the situation. She bit her lip.

Troy's expression flickered, a mixture of surprise and something deeper that Blue couldn't quite decipher. He seemed to be wrestling with his own thoughts, his emotions mirroring the conflict that raged within her.

"I know there are rumours, whispers, secrets that everyone loves to discuss," Troy finally spoke, his voice laced with a hint of defensiveness. "it's a small village, close knit. But that doesn't mean they're grounded in any truth. There's more to my family's history than what she may have heard."

Blue nodded slowly, her gaze holding his. She knew him, knew he cared, knew the bond they had forged. But in the face of uncertainty, her loyalty to Jess and the need to uncover the truth remained firm.

Blue's heart carried a hidden truth that even she struggled to confront. She had buried it away. Her feelings for Troy ran deeper than she cared to admit. Their shared moments, the laughter, the quiet conversations under the stars. She had spent so much time in his arms, she knew the contours of his body like she knew the back of her hand. It was like they were two halves of one whole. She just couldn't deny it any longer; she had tried and failed. But, as much as she wanted to acknowledge this feeling of love, Jessie's warnings and the dark secrets that seemed to taint his family's history cast a shadow of doubt over her. Blue was torn between the growing love she felt and the unsettling truths that lay hidden, dug in, laying in the dark, beneath the surface.

It was his aunt though, his aunt with her cold, unfeeling ways. That's what really made her blood run cold and her mind put up barriers.

Eliza Calete's reputation cast a long shadow over Celestia, a presence that invoked fear and unease among the inhabitants of Hallowed Brook. Her aura was one of mystery, icy command and sternness, an unusual and enigmatic figure whose cold presence and difficult nature were well-known throughout the whole valley. The whispers of her actions and the rumours of her involvement in the darker aspects of the Calete family business only added to the grim murkiness that muddied her name. Among the residents of Celestia, especially within the Brook, there was a collective wariness around Eliza, a deep-seated knowledge that her intentions were dark, that they were often veiled in secrecy, and that crossing paths with her could have dire consequences.

She had seen something else, something in the sketchbooks, something she hadn't mentioned to anyone yet, something eerie that pointed to Eliza Calete having a strange link to Jess.

Blue knew that it was time to get her own answers.

CHAPTER 18

TROY

"What about Eliza?" Blue's question hung like fog in the air; Troy recognised her tone. She was judging his aunt, many did. There was something else under it too: she knew something.

As Troy's troubled eyes flashed, she turned her gaze intently upon him, probing with her blue pools. Troy's stare met hers, his tired eyes reflecting the heaviness of the secrets he carried. He felt like he was being buried in the dirt, buried and left to rot.

"Eliza... she's not an easy person to explain. She's my aunt, yes, but there's...more to her than that. Her link with the Capital Core...and..." His low voice stuttered; it was laced with hesitation. He was grappling with his own conflicted feelings about his family. About his Aunt Eliza. Truth be told he was suspicious of her too.

He watched Blue's brow furrow as she studied him. Something softened within him.

"You don't have to say anything, to tell us, we can't make you, not at all Troy, but this is Jess, this is our best friend."

Troy heaved a heavy sigh, his fingers absentmindedly twisting. His eyes closed. The confident Troy who ran the fields, kept the foragers in line, he had disappeared. Blown away with the wind.

"It's just... Eliza has always been a mystery, even to me. She's ambitious, driven. We've always owned the land around here, and yes there's a darkness that lingers in the shadows of our family's past. Lately, with the pressure to supply more to the Capital Core, Eliza's actions have been..." He paused, searching for the right words. "Unpredictable, to say the least."

Troy's mind felt mired in the very dirt they raked through, torn between the weight of the secrets he kept within and the urgency of finding Jess, of helping the woman he loved find peace.

"What's your plan?" He asked, changing the subject from the dusty cobwebs, the skeletons that lurked in his family's cupboards.

Hell, please let her be alive.

He listened intently as Ky and Blue exchanged ideas, their faces etched with tenuous threads of hope.

"Because of the map, the sketches, we're planning on venturing into the Desire Mountains, up to Lumina Lake. Just below the Atlas peak. It'll take a good few hours, maybe longer," Ky said.

"It was a place that was often mentioned in her scrapbook, and it was circled on the map, I just feel it's a starting point, somewhere we could begin," Blue explained.

"But Blue you need to be careful. Your back... your pain... and, it's dangerous... there are vicious creatures up there, ones that we know nothing about," Troy added anxiously. He sighed, cursing. The prospect of them seeking answers in that uncharted terrain, seemed both daunting and reckless.

"We don't have a choice," it was Blue. She looked at him, the adamant gaze showed him there was no budging her. No trying to change her mind.

Troy's brain grappled with the web of secrets he had inadvertently unravelled. He regretted the digging he had done. The dirt he now knew. He couldn't afford to let Blue or Ky know about the details of his furtive meeting with Titus, no matter what. The Visionary couldn't speak of his secrets, of that he was pretty sure. That was something he clung to, a fragile oath protecting him. Protecting the family business. His father.

But Troy felt himself becoming numb, his mind gritty, filled to the brim with fine gravel. Turning him to stone. Visiting Titus had indeed set in motion a chain of events that Troy could feel spiralling beyond his control. The cloying pressure of his family's secrets, the pressure of protecting those he cared for, and now pressure to find Jess, had all come together, leaving him with a perplexing decision to make. The trouble was he was paralysed with fear, afraid of creating more catastrophe. As he replayed the events in his mind, he couldn't help but wonder if there could be another option, a different path they could take, a better plan.

"Do you have another way buddy? We're all ears…" Ky asked almost like he was reading Troy's mind.

But deep in his heart, Troy knew that their choices were limited. The desperation to uncover the truth about Jessie's disappearance had driven him to seek guidance from Titus, as was traditional. The secrets he had shared, the revelations about his family's past, well it had all been a calculated risk, a leap of faith in the hopes of finding his dear friend. And, of making Blue smile again. But, had it been a mistake?

He shook his head.

"No, I don't," he answered as he lowered his eyes and sighed.

As he stood poised upon a high precipice, rooted to the spot with uncertainty, Troy grappled with the consequences of his actions. Fear clawed at him, threatening to overwhelm his resolve. He knew that he had acted out of necessity, out of the deep-seated need to unravel the mystery that had gripped their lives. But he was terrified that this could make everything come falling down like a deadly landslide.

"Troy we need time. Blue and I need to take time off from work in the fields, we have to go in daylight."

"I know things in Elysium Fields are strained Troy, that we have hungry mouths to feed across the planet, but Jessie, she needs us. Blue's right, we should have acted a long time ago. What were we even thinking?"

Troy weighed their words carefully. The tension between his aunt's demands and the desire to solve the puzzle of Jessie's disappearance was obvious, but the urgency of the situation required action. They were right. With a heavy sigh, he nodded in agreement, his voice firm again.

"Alright, you two can take the time off," he conceded. "We'll manage the work somehow."

The giant loomed above them. A wise look upon his aged face suggesting that his intentions here had been fulfilled. Troy's irritation flared; he didn't want to feel angry, but he did. Was he being played? Everything was getting more mired in mud, his life was tangled in enough roots of deceit, he didn't need more pulling him underground.

The Visionary's strident voice boomed, "I'll return to my place in the rocky outcrop with Ryoni and seek the guidance of the spirits for your safe return."

Troy choked down his irritation, it wasn't helpful, and deep within him he was convinced that this was all part of the twisting path that the spirits had laid out for them.

As Troy prepared to head back, a sudden realisation struck him. He turned to Blue and Ky, determination glowing in his eyes.

"Wait there. Before you go, I need to speak with Eliza. I'm going to tell her that I'm coming with you."

With that decision firmly made, Troy knew that his journey into the Desire Mountains was not just about finding Jess, but about confronting the truths that had remained hidden within his family for far too long. He wanted to face the darkness head on.

"But… Eliza…the Capital Core…" Blue breathed looking ashen.

Troy took a deep breath, finding his voice amidst the twisting turmoil within him.

"Look, it's true, you both have a point. We can't afford to stand still, waiting for something to change. Lumina Lake might hold some answers. I have to come with you. I have to… I owe it to Jess," he glanced at Ky and Blue, his gaze revealing the conflict he felt. "We can take a break from the fields, dig for food later. I'll talk to Eliza about it. I'll tell her."

As the words tripped off his tongue, he simultaneously thrummed with trepidation and tenacity. The decision to tell his aunt about the trek was a risky one, yet he knew that he couldn't just take off without informing her, especially not now.

With a final glance at Ky, Blue, and Titus, Troy turned and headed towards his family's tree house.

"Please... Troy...Don't tell her why or where. Keep that to yourself," Jess shouted after him. "Please, just trust me on this. Tell her there's something you have to do but, promise me you won't give her specifics. And I beg you Troy, please don't mention Jess. It's important."

She looked pale, anxiety written all over her face, her mouth set into a thin, grave line.

"Okay," he replied, looking back over his shoulder. He felt his stomach sinking, his legs trembling.

What exactly had Blue discovered?

CHAPTER 19

JESS

The voice was familiar. She desperately tried to make sense of who was standing in front of her, whose heels were clattering across the stone. The hood they had thrust over her face made her lightheaded, she was nauseous, and her legs shook as she sat shivering on the cold, stone floor. Her brain wouldn't allow her to make sense of who was behind those words.

The Droids had arrived earlier, their commands blunt, their hold on her firm. Why was their demeanour different again? Without explanation, they had placed her in another room. Yet another cave. An empty, obsidian black cave. It was like mind games.

Were they purposely trying to disorientate her? Were they employing torture methods before they killed her? Was this her executioner, menacingly pacing the floor?

She had heard one word, "Leave."

In that single utterance a thousand jumbled thoughts and questions made her dizzy. Jess was reaching breaking point. But, she knew that's exactly what they wanted, that was the aim.

"Why are you here?" Came the sudden question, Jess was sure the woman was standing right behind her. The shock made her stomach lurch; she almost gagged. Swallowing down the bile, she wracked her brains for the

121

right response. Her memories circled.

"I...I... don't know."

"Liar!" The reply was like a slap.

"I swear. I'm not lying, I don't know..." her voice, muffled by the hood sounded so frail, so weak. Jess hated the sound. It sounded nothing like her. She had lost an integral part of her in these caves.

"You saw something... didn't you?"

Jessie's breath hitched and her brain screeched. Whose voice was that?

"I... I don't understand... please...what do you mean?"

The silence was dense and filled with nightmarish imaginings. It stretched and became like a living, breathing tormentor.

***

Jess awoke with a start; her arms were numb and for a second, she had forgotten exactly where she was. The reality came rushing back with a power that threatened to suffocate her.

In the depths of yet another cave, Jess listened to the scurrying noises, the scratches and strange sounds of creatures that slunk about in the pitch black. The icy cold of the stone floor, seemed to seep into her bones, while the hood over her head completely obscured her surroundings. Her bound hands, though now only loosely tied, left her feeling vulnerable and confined. In her mind there was an itch, like a freshly healed scab that demanded scratching, her thoughts kept returning to the insistent prickle. She knew that voice. She sat and waited. Waiting in the dark, waiting with bated breath, waiting with that continual itch.

When she had suspected there would be no more questions, a vaguely familiar voice echoed through the space, a harsh voiced woman whose identity remained elusive. Jess sensed an iciness in the tone that made her shiver. The disorientation added to Jess's growing unease. Again, there was the rhythmic sound of high heels pacing the room, the thuds seemed to echo the frantic beat of her fluttering heart.

The woman's questions were relentless, each one designed to chip away at Jess's defences.

"What did you see?" The repeated words hung in the air, and Jess's voice wavered as she replied, "I don't know... I've told you... I don't." The lengthening, infinite silence that followed was as unsettling as the questions themselves, another tactic to fray her nerves.

Who was it?

She counted. A continual repetition in her head, one to a hundred, over and over. Amidst the quiet, a whisper brushed against Jessie's ear, causing her to tense. A scent filled her nostrils, an earthy, pine scent that reminded her of home. She pictured a small batlike creature, like a little ball of black was hovering by her ear.

"What did you see in The Capital Core?" The question hit her like a revelation, the pieces clattering, falling into place. A light bulb moment blinding her. It was all connected. This was about the toxic waste, the room full of Droids laden with bulky containers for Calete Company, the containers that had been labelled Lumina Lake. The containers they'd been asked to collect. Destined for their main source of water. The dots joined together, revealing a chilling truth that sent shivers down her spine.

Eliza.

It was Eliza Calete, Troy's aunt. Essentially the head of the company she worked for. Bile rose in her throat once more; the bitterness made her gag.

The woman's intent became clearer, her inquiries tied to the dark underbelly of Celestia, to secrets hidden beneath layers of deception. To the dirt that had begun to kill off their animals, no doubt poisoned the Brook and made many across Celestia sick. Sick with weak bones and continual gnawing pain, Blue was one of them.

"What do you know? Tell me."

It was like the words were actually inside her brain, like they were etched into her brain like the drawings she had etched upon the stone.

"Nothing…I know nothing Eliza." As soon as she said the word, the name of her captor she knew it was a mistake. A huge mistake.

The silence stretched and stretched, it became almost like a living, breathing thing. As Jess grappled with the enormity of what she had said, how her knowledge could end her life, she tried hard not to weep.

The confinement of the cave felt even more suffocating. Her mind darted and flitted, her thoughts tangled up with fragments of information that screeched to be understood. But amidst the uncertainty, one thing was clear. She was here for a reason. She had been purposely captured. She was being silenced. The dirt path she had unknowingly stumbled across was a path fraught with danger, leading her deeper into tunnels of corruption and bleakness. This knowledge threatened not only her safety but the safety of everyone she held dear. The whole of Hallowed Brook.

***

Eliza had gone. Vanished. Without revealing herself from the shadows, she had left Jess all alone with her thoughts. As Jess continued to sit, bound and reeling in the dim cave, she fought to shield herself from the terrifying grip of her surroundings, attempting to drown out the last few hours, the unsettling presence of Eliza Calete. The realisation that this cold-hearted woman was behind the pollution that was plaguing their land, hit Jess like a blow, stirring a potent mix of anger, disbelief and sorrow.

How could she poison her own town? Her own land?

Beyond harming water and food supplies, the devastation extended to the extraordinary flora and fauna that usually thrived in The Desire Mountains. And, the people.

Vivid memories of what she had begun to witness flooded Jess's mind. The lifeless forms of once-vibrant Sue Sue birds, wild tree creatures, Bananoos, twisted by unnatural deformities, a Saint Blurt marred by painful sores. Each image carved a fissure into her heart, a wound that bled due to the havoc that Eliza's actions had wreaked. The elements came together, formed a clear picture in her mind, a haunting realisation that the barrels of tainted dirt were the root cause.

In the face of the cave's oppressive, caustic silence, Jess clung to a fierce determination. Her love of the land, the creatures, and the spirit of Celestia fuelled her resolve. She knew that exposing Eliza's cruelty was essential not just for her own survival, but for the preservation of the delicate balance that sustained their part of Celestia. As she navigated the shadows of the cave, Jess vowed to uncover the truth, the truth she needed to expose, the truth that would unveil the murky web of corruption that threatened to bury the very wonder of the planet she held dear. Truth. This is what encouraged her to stay alive, to keep breathing.

CHAPTER 20

THE VISIONARY

As Titus Cariad and his Shadow Wolf Ryoni made their way back up into the higher reaches of the valley, back to their wooden hut, a sense of satisfaction seemed to settle within him. The giant had managed to persuade the friends to begin a search for Jess, this was a move towards the hidden truth that they all sought. And Troy, he should find some relief too, he mused.

Yet, as they were halfway into their upward climb, amidst the serenity, an unexpected sight caught the giant's attention. It was fleeting, he almost missed it. A matt-black, peculiar object hidden among the foliage. Red lights flashed. Titus' brow furrowed as he recognised the telltale signs of a Droid. This was most puzzling. These rare mechanical beings were never seen beyond the Capital Core. What was a machine designed to perform hazardous tasks in the Capital doing here within the valley? His huge brow furrowed; the Droid's unexpected presence was deeply concerning.

Determined to investigate, Titus moved closer, his instincts urging him to uncover the mystery behind the machine's appearance. His meaty hand grabbed the staff tightly, using the Visitotem to part the long grass.

However, before he could properly react, the Droid swiftly burrowed into the ground, disappearing from view. The Visionary's confusion deepened, as his connection to the spirits failed to provide any answers to this curious event. He heard only the rustle of the bushes, the swaying of the trees. He banged his Visitotem upon the mossy ground in frustration. Should he dig it out?

Damned Droids.

He disliked the unnatural creatures. Being man made, they were an enigma, he felt zero connection with the emotionless machines made to do the dirty jobs that Celestians didn't want to. He couldn't read them and that made him suspicious.

Why was a worker Droid, an expensive litter picker, to all intents and purposes, all the way over in this part of the planet? Especially when only certain places were licences to use such technology.

But Titus Cariad's attention was soon diverted as Ryoni, his vulpine companion, showed sudden signs of distress. He collapsed. The speed of the Shadow Wolf's illness was alarming, his usually vibrant energy was replaced by a destabilising lethargy in the mere blink of an eye. He tried to stand with fearful, glassy eyes. The wolf's mouth frothed with foamy saliva and his gait was unsteady. He flopped to the floor again.

"Hey, hey...what's the matter?"

Panic surged through Titus as he realised the urgency of the situation. He knew that the powers of the spirits would help him, and he wasted no time in trying to channel their healing energy.

"Spirits...gather and give me strength."

Titus scooped Ryoni from the muddy ground and sprinted up the mountain side, his thundering strides causing trees to shake and animals to flee. His mind was blank, saving Ryoni his only care.

Within his hut, the giant set to work, combining his knowledge of spells with the otherworldly power he could harness. The room filled with an eerie glow as Titus channelled his connection to the spirits, infusing the potion he prepared with their healing essence. With every incantation and gesture, he poured his energy into the concoction, a desperate plea for Ryoni's well-being and a fervent hope that his efforts, supported by the spirits, would revive the inert wolf.

As the healing potion took shape, Titus Cariad's fervour was strengthened. The spirits' presence, once again summoned to aid him, provided a glimmer of hope in the face of uncertainty. With each passing moment, he poured his energy into the spell, hoping that the bond he shared with Ryoni and the power of the spirits combined would be enough to restore his beloved companion to health.

"Spirits of ancient realms, hear my call. With the essence of earth, air, fire, and water, I beseech you to heal. Flow through me, let your energy mend what's broken. Illuminate the shadows that ail my companion, Ryoni."

He stared at the prone Shadow Wolf.

"By the power of the elements, by the force of unity, I invoke your presence.

Stitch together his vitality, restore his strength. Let his spirit shine, renewed and invigorated. By my trust in your power, I implore you to mend, to nurture, to revive.

As the connection between us defies boundaries,

let your energy bridge the gap. Breathe life into Ryoni, restoring his well-being. With humility and hope, I present my plea. Manifest your healing essence and guide him back to health. So be it."

As the incantation's echoes faded, a subtle shift rippled through the air. Ryoni, the loyal Shadow Wolf, began to stir, his once-glassy eyes regaining a glimmer of consciousness. However, the spark of life that returned to him was fragile, his heartbeat feeble as if struggling to regain its rhythm. Titus watched with a mixture of relief and concern, the love between them palpable.

Ryoni's movements were sluggish, a sign of his weakened state. The healing energy had begun its work, but it was clear that he required more than just the power of the spirits. Titus gently cradled the Shadow Wolf, his giant hands carefully supporting the creature's body. He could feel the delicate thump of Ryoni's heart against his palm, a reminder of the fragility of his life, a life that teetered on the edge.

A sense of urgency swelled within Titus as he considered the cause of Ryoni's sudden collapse. Could the encounter with the Droid have triggered this sickness? Could it have carried a bacteria from the capital? The thought weighed heavily on his mind; an alarming insistent repetitive question that refused to be silenced.

The Visionary's brow furrowed as he grappled with the possibility, his concern for Ryoni's well-being was intertwined with his determination to uncover the truth behind this perplexing situation. More hidden mysteries, more conundrums. He was at the end of his tether, his serenity at rock bottom.

Gently cradling Ryoni in his arms, Titus carried him to a comfortable spot within the hut. With a tender touch, he settled the Shadow Wolf onto a soft cushion, before covering him with a crochet blanket. Then he brooded, watching as the creature began to drift into a restful slumber. The giant's mind remained alert, his instincts urging him to delve deeper, to linger on the many questions that now hung in the air. Titus felt that this was a mystery that held the key not only to Ryoni's sudden sickness but to the broader web of intrigue that was slowly unravelling within their world. Celestia was a small planet, it was odd that things seemed off kilter all of a sudden.

Stepping outside his hut, Titus Cariad cast his gaze skyward, seeking solace and answers in the embrace of the night. Trying to meditate before he allowed the pinpricks in the heavens to fill his mind. Yet, what met his eyes was far from the serene expanse of stars he had hoped for. He gasped and his lilac eyes widened. Instead, a disheartening sight greeted him. Like an omen, an eerie ribbon of brown, a smog-like veil tainted the air. The acrid scent that reached his nostrils was a visceral reminder of pollution's unwelcome presence.

His chest tightened, and a deep furrow creased his brow as he took in the sight before him. This was no ordinary celestial display; it was a sign of contamination, a sombre smear upon the usually perfect canvas of the night. A dirty smudge. Confusion danced in his lilac eyes as he contemplated the connection between the smog's appearance and the bizarre events that had unfolded this evening: Ryoni's inexplicable collapse, the mysterious Droid, and the weird disappearance of Jess.

Titus pondered the threads that might weave these separate events into a single tapestry, a story of what was happening here on Celestia. Could the Droid's arrival in Hallowed Brook have triggered not only Ryoni's condition but also this unrelenting smog that choked the night air? Were these events somehow intertwined, part of a grimmer scheme that extended beyond their knowledge? And most importantly, could they be linked to the woman Jessie and her worrying vanishing act? The thick foggy air seemed like a warning that held a vital clue to the unfolding mystery.

As the Visionary stood beneath the tainted night sky, his determination surged. With Ryoni's well-being on the line and the shadow of Jess's disappearance casting darkness over Hallowed Brook, he knew that he must unravel the intricacies that connected all that plagued the area. Guided by his unyielding bond with the land and the spirits, he resolved to seek answers, no matter how dark, no matter how far underground and no matter how twisted the truth may be.

CHAPTER 21

BLUE

Blue's thoughts were consumed by the looming journey ahead as she brooded in the quiet embrace of her treehouse. She felt conflicted. Determination coursed through her veins, mingled with a cautious optimism that they might uncover something about Jess and her disappearance but there was also a dread that she could be lost forever. It didn't bear thinking about.

The luminescent hues of twilight decorated the open sky outside her window, casting a gossamer glow that entranced her.

As she prepared for bed, her fingers brushed the soft fur of Scruffy, her loyal tree cat, seeking comfort in the presence of her silent companion.

She made a herbal tea and sat on her circular bed. Before she slipped into a deep slumber, before she dreamt those kaleidoscopic, vivid dreams, a whisper of intuition guided her steps across the suspension bridge to Jessie's nearby treehouse. The bridge that had always linked them. The bridge that now felt like the opening to a tomb. The air held a faint scent of nostalgia as she entered the bright, cozy space. Memories of laughter, shared secrets, and quiet moments flooded her mind again as she stared around at Jess' things.

To Blue, the weight of her absence became like a

barrel, pressing down persistently upon her heart.

She sat and soaked in the lost essence of her friend. A noise startled her, and she dropped her cup. Reaching for it, beneath the small sofa, her fingers brushed against a forgotten canvas. Curiosity aroused, she carefully retrieved it, her breath catching as the painting came into view. The scene that greeted her was jarring, a stark contrast to the vibrant world they knew. Hallowed Brook, once a sanctuary of life, growth and coexistence, lay devastated in the artwork's depiction. Totally destroyed.

Her gaze traced the cracked earth, barren and desolate, the once-thriving trees reduced to skeletal remains. Thick, suffocating pollution hung in the air, a gauzy shroud that choked the landscape. The imagery held an eerie familiarity, mirroring the smog she had witnessed earlier. And there, written in Jessie's sloping handwriting, were words that resonated with an unsettling truth: "How long until this land is lost?"

They had already poisoned the waters of the Brook and polluted Elysium Fields.

A chill crept down Blue's spine as she grappled with the implications of the painting. What had Jess seen? What had she feared? What was harming their corner of the planet? The artwork seemed to hold a dire warning, a glimpse into a potential future that sent shivers down Blue's spine. As she clutched the eerie canvas, the need to do something only deepened. She would uncover the truth behind Jessie's vanishing, no matter what ugly darkness lay ahead.

With the weight of the painting and its message causing her to catch her breath, she drifted into a restless, heavy sleep. There in her best friend's treehouse. As she slept, her dreams were haunted by the fragile beauty of Hallowed Brook, The meandering Desire Mountains and the whole of Celestia, she wallowed in muddy pits, screaming up into a brown smudged sky. Her mind conjured a nightmarish future and the secrets and lies that needed unearthing danced upon the edges of her subconscious.

At some point in the night, she had left the lucid dreams, tiptoed back to her own bed, to Scruffy and the connections that bound her to the here and now. She grounded herself back in reality.

Blue awoke early, a hum of adrenaline coursing through her veins. With a determined exhale, she swung her legs over the side of her circular bed, her feet meeting the cool, wooden floorboards with a soft thud. Scruffy was by her side, stretching and meeping. The early hour held a silent stillness that resonated within her, a moment of pause, a calm before the day's journey swept her up into its storm.

As Blue rose to her feet, the millions of thoughts that had once raced through her mind began to settle into a singular focus: Jess, Lumina Lake, the unfolding truth.

With a wistful sigh, she dressed, gathered up her belongings and slung her bag over her shoulder, ready to step into the unknown and face whatever challenges lay ahead.

The ache in Blue's back throbbed in constant protest, a reminder of the physical challenges she would face during their trek to Lumina Lake. She hoped the layers she wore would keep her warm.

As she prepared to climb down the rungs, into the muddy meadow, she couldn't help but cast a glance at Scruffy, her faithful companion, curled up peacefully upon the bed.

"I'll be back soon Mr Scruff," she promised.

She stole a final glance around the cosy treehouse. The familiarity of her surroundings brought a bittersweet comfort, a silent reminder of the life she was leaving behind, if only temporarily.

"Hopefully, I'll be returning with Jess in tow," she smiled. Who was she trying to convince?

With each downward step, Blue worried that she was purposely lowering herself into a tunnel of despair.

CHAPTER 22

TROY

Troy's steps carried him through the bustling fields of Hallowed Brook, his chest heavy with the weight of his deceptive words. Words that added to the already tangled web of lies. They sat like grit upon his tongue. The fabricated tale of a healing herb, a herb for Blue's back, and a journey to the southerly regions, was meant to mislead Eliza Calete, to buy them the time they needed for their true undertaking. But even as he approached her treehouse, an unsettling feeling gnawed at his gut. He felt eyes were watching him. An unsettling feeling in the pit of his stomach made him glance over his shoulder. The imposing Calete treehouse was empty, silent. She wasn't there. The relief that flooded him was palpable.

Leaving a note to explain their absence, Troy felt a mixture of apprehension and a lifting of a heavy weight upon his shoulders. He hadn't wanted to face her. If she came at him with those thinly veiled threats about his father again, he wasn't sure if he could contain his explosive anger. Still, he was uncertain of what her reaction might be when she discovered their ruse. What she would do then. Restlessness tugged at him as he made his way back to his own treehouse, only to be greeted by the Lunafi's antics. The creature's mischief and her growing appetite were becoming as tiresome as they were humorous. He was pleased to see her on the mend.

As the day melted into evening, Troy packed a bag with careful consideration, his mind divided between his longing to be with Blue and the responsibility he felt for the endearing, little creature that he had given refuge within his treehouse. Despite his unease, exhaustion eventually claimed him, pulling him into a world of tumbling, tangled dreams.

Nightmares danced on the edges of his mind, their unsettling threads twisting into a tapestry of darkness. A darkness that seemed to hold a mirror up to the tangled shroud of secrets that cloaked him. A mirror that reflected his grimy ancestry. A thousand shadowy Caletes.

Then he dreamt of Blue. Of stolen kisses, of holding her in his arms, of the heat that simmered between them. The dream made him sweat, twisting with longing.

He awoke with a start, his heart racing as he felt the weight of the Lunafi nestled and purring upon his chest. The animal's presence comforted him and confined him, a blunt reminder that he couldn't just leave Luna behind.

Oh no! He mused, now he'd even named her.

With a sigh, Troy fashioned a makeshift carrier for the Lunafi, resolving to bring the creature along on the journey. As the morning sun painted the sky with hues of gold that pierced and shattered the smoky grey, Troy found himself in the Hallowed Brook meeting place, where Ky's infectious humour rang shrilly in the air. The jovial chatter was a stark contrast to the heaviness he felt about their journey, and yet, he grasped it, as it offered a fleeting break from the worries that weighed him down. He smiled, despite himself.

"Ready to embark on this grand adventure, eh?" Ky's voice rang out with a light-heartedness that Troy couldn't help but be infected by.

He paused, exchanging a meaningful glance with Blue. How he wanted to hold her in that moment, to gain some strength from her embrace. Her drawn expression didn't escape his notice, and a pang of concern tightened his chest. He should have gone to her last night. He cursed his cowardice.

"What's got you looking so serious, Blue? This journey's meant to be your chance to see what lies beyond, see the things that Jess loved whilst we search," Ky said.

Blue's lips curved into a small smile, though the worry still lingered in her eyes. "I know, Ky. It's just... well, sometimes the unknown can be more daunting than thrilling. Besides, I'm aching already. Surely, I'm not the only one wondering how we're going to try to make sense of all of this... of a path to Jess."

Troy nodded, his eyes meeting hers, drowning in the blue. Desperate to kiss her. His own thoughts echoed Blue's sentiments. They were about to step into the icy upper reaches, to follow the trail left behind by Jess, and in doing so, they were diving headfirst into a mystery that could change everything. As Blue and Troy exchanged glances, a silent understanding passed between them, a shared message of support.

Ky chuckled, clapping Troy on the back. "Ah, come on, my friends! Adventure is what life's all about. And besides, you've got me as your trusty guide. What on earth could possibly go wrong?"

Troy's lips twitched in a half-smile, the friendship that

they shared offering a brief reprieve from the gravity of their quest.

"Ky, listen, I've known you long enough to know that when you're involved, 'what could go wrong?' is usually just the beginning of a messy, unforgettable tale. It doesn't fill me with confidence Buddy."

Blue's tinkling laughter mingled with Ky's, a shared moment of lightness that seemed to pierce through the anxiety that had been lingering, cloaking them all. "I'm not going to lie. You've got a point there, Troy," she chimed in, her smile a mixture of affection and agreement.

"I was thinking exactly the same Ky. But let's just hope this unforgettable tale has a fairytale ending. We need a happily ever after right now."

As they shared more laughter and teasing, playful conversation, the tension in the air began to steadily ease, being replaced by an urge to get started on their journey. Troy realised that they might be stepping into the unknown, facing dangers and secrets that they couldn't fully comprehend, but they were doing it together. And in that shared bond, they would find strength. To Troy, the promise of adventure, as well as the hope that they could bring Jess home, uncover the truth that had been blanketed in shady darkness for far too long and explore parts of their land where they had never been, seemed almost worth the coiling worry in his guts.

He looked up as Blue's curious gaze fell upon the small, silver furred Lunafi nestled among his belongings. Her brows raised in surprise, and a mixture of amusement and concern danced in her eyes.

"Hey, who and what is this?" she asked, a bemused

smile tugging at the corners of her lips.

Troy's expression softened as he looked down at the Lunafi, his voice gentle as he answered, "Oh, her? She's Luna, a wounded Lunafi I found the other day. Figured she could use a bit of adventure too."

Luna's silvery, indigo fur glinted in the morning light as she blinked up at Blue, her amber eyes wide and curious. Blue chuckled, her heart clearly warmed by the sight of the tiny creature.

"Aren't they meant to be magical? I heard they can ward off evil. Anyway, nice to meet you Luna, welcome to our motley crew. I hope you don't mind the cold little one."

Ky's laughter ricocheted off the meeting place's wooden walls, his eyes twinkling with genuine mirth. He shook his head.

"A wounded Lunafi, eh? Buddy, for real? You sure know how to pick 'em, Troy."

Troy's lips curled into a wry smile.

" Yeah, yeah...I couldn't leave her behind. And who knows, Ky? Maybe they are like an amulet, deflecting malevolence, that's what people say about them right?

Perhaps Luna's luck in finding me will bring us some good fortune on this journey. I'm keeping positive," he grinned.

As the trio shared a light-hearted moment, a sense of togetherness grew between them, a togetherness that helped push aside the weight of their worries, if only for a fleeting moment. Ky's voice broke through the tinkling laughter. "Alright, alright, enough standing around. Let's go...Time to hit the trail, adventurers. I hope you've brought snacks."

Blue nodded, her smile directed at Troy, something unspoken clear in her azure eyes.

"He's right. Besides, all this standing about is making my back screech with pain. And yes Ky, I've got some fine dried shield bugs... want one?"

With a lightness that he'd not felt for a very long time, Troy gathered his belongings, took one last lingering look around the Brook, then began the upward climb. the unknown stretching before them, a landscape waiting to be explored. And as the first few hundred metres of their journey got underway, the Lunafi, Luna, tucked safely among them, he couldn't help but feel a twinge of tentative excitement, a flicker of hope for what lay ahead.

The pulsing red lasers completely escaped his notice.

CHAPTER 23

JESS

Jess awoke to the distant calls of the mighty Devout Drolle, its plaintive cries echoing through the cave. The usually majestic sounds had taken on an urgent and stressed tone, causing a shiver to run down her spine. As she lay on the thin mattress in the dimly lit cave, she couldn't help but wonder what could be causing such a marked change in the bird's behaviour.

The memory of her encounter with Eliza Calete lingered in her mind like a dark cloud. The woman's voice, sharp and cold, had questioned her relentlessly. Over and over. Until she had wanted to scratch at her ears to stop the noise.

"What did you see?" she had demanded, her tone cutting through the air like a knife.

Jess sighed, trying to block out the memory, her fingers tracing the rough texture of the cave walls. She knew that Eliza was involved in something corrupt, something that had to do with the barrels of dirt she had seen. To do with the Droids. The Saint Blurt's hooves reverberated through the cave, a reminder of the world she was separated from.

She shifted her gaze upward, her heart sinking as she saw the crack in the cave's ceiling. Through the opening, she caught a glimpse of an unusual brown smog that tainted the once clear sky. The air felt thick and caustic, assaulting her senses as she struggled to breathe. A sudden bout of coughing doubled her over, the acrid smell of pollution infiltrated her lungs. Her eye stung.

As the realisation dawned upon her, Jess felt a surge of anger and fear. Whatever was happening outside was connected to what she had seen. What she knew. She couldn't help but feel that her discovery had put her in danger, that she had stumbled upon a secret that powerful forces were to protect by any means necessary. But even as fear gripped her, a stubborn determination also rose within her. She wouldn't back down, she wouldn't let fear silence her. She would find a way to expose the truth and protect the world she loved, no matter the cost.

Unable to be stilled, her mind raced as she lay in the cave, grappling with her thoughts and fears. The events Jess had witnessed and the pieces of the puzzle she had now gathered all seemed to lead to one inescapable truth: something was terribly wrong with their world, and someone powerful was responsible for it.

She couldn't help but wonder if Troy had any inkling of what was happening. He was her friend, after all, and surely, he wouldn't stand by and let their company destroy Hallowed Brook and the beauty of Celestia itself. She had seen the devastating effects of whatever was going on firsthand. The polluted river, the ecologically dead waters tainted by some kind of toxicity. The thought of their once-pristine environment being irreversibly damaged weighed heavily on her heart.

Her mind drifted to Lumina Lake, a place of tranquillity and beauty that had been forever changed by something man made. She had witnessed the shift in its colours, the crystal-clear blue giving way to a sickly, swampy green. She remembered the trickling ebb and flow of the water, the very source of life, now thick and foul, making her stomach churn. She had been forced to drink it, to consume the very poison that was spreading across their land. The thought made her sick.

Jess clenched her fists, her resolve hardening. She wouldn't let fear and helplessness consume her. She wouldn't let those responsible for the destruction of her world go unpunished. With a determined fire in her belly, she vowed to find a way to expose the truth, to stop the pollution, and to save Celestia from the grasp of those who sought to exploit it for their own gain. She had to get out of here, find a path, so that she could protect the planet she loved.

In the dimness of the cave, Jess's senses were on high alert. A faint sound danced on the edge of her consciousness, a sound that seemed out of place in the midst of her captivity. She strained to listen, her heart racing as she thought she heard Blue's tinkling laughter carried by the wind. But it couldn't be true, could it? Blue's laughter was a memory of happier times, a stark contrast to the bleak situation she found herself in now. She must be imagining it.

Doubt and disbelief warred within her, her mind returning to the idea that her friend could be nearby. Yet, it seemed too impossible, too good to be true. Eliza Calete's cruel tactics during the interrogation had left her feeling fragile and vulnerable, unsure of who she could trust. Was she playing with her? Was her own head still battling the evil of Eliza and her corruption?

Exhaustion, both physical and emotional, weighed heavily on her shoulders. The events of the previous day had taken a toll on her, leaving Jess drained and weary. As her racing thoughts gradually quietened, she found herself slipping back into a fitful sleep, her dreams haunted by shadows of uncertainty and the looming threat of disaster that hung over her world.

In her dreams a warning rang clear:

Beware what has been buried.

CHAPTER 24

THE VISIONARY

The Visionary stared at the ingredients he had gathered as he exhaled a loud, worry-filled sigh. A sigh that made Ryoni jump from his resting place in the corner. Titus Cariad's head was heavy with unanswered questions, his brow furrowed, his mind filled with a myriad of dark, ever spiralling thoughts.

Looking upwards, out of a window in the roof of his hut, he nervously observed the ominous changes in the sky. Pausing, he watched the wispy, potent smog that blanketed the once clear air. Was this a grim sign of pollution that could further destroy their land or was this connected to some dark, malicious force?

As he tended to Ryoni, watching over his loyal Wolf with worry plain in his lilac eyes, he couldn't shake the insistent alarm, the urgency that was burning, coursing around his veins with a fiery intensity. He needed to act.

With the health of the land and its inhabitants at stake, he knew he had to find a way to halt the spreading toxicity, he had to find it quickly. With his gut roiling in trepidation, he mulled over the news that had travelled his way. News of people falling ill in other parts of Celestia. These details had reached him from other Visionaries, carried via messenger Croaks, the birds had proffered scrolls, their contents shaking him to the core. This disquieting knowledge only heightened his desire to come up with a way to make things right.

With a start, he realised that he had forgotten to ask the spirits for protection for Ky, Blue, and Troy. He had been so caught up in the need to heal Ryoni. But he understood now, it was transparently clear, beyond the missing girl from Hallowed Brook, he had a larger battle to fight here. This was a critical battle against some sort of toxic contamination that was spreading, infecting everything around the Hallowed Brook area like a deadly disease. He feared it had heinous origins. Had he missed the signs? Or had he been purposely blocked from seeing the truth?

Summoning his connection to the spirits once more, he called upon their divine guidance and power. He knew he needed to use the assembled ingredients to create a potent potion that could cleanse the air and prevent their land coming to any further harm. To protect the magical animals that called this valley home. He thought about Jessie then...of what Troy had revealed. Had someone hurt his Shadow Wolf on purpose?

With Ryoni's condition showing significant signs of improvement, he set to work, channelling his energy and weaving his spells to create a potion that could hopefully disperse the smog and restore the precious purity of the Brook's air. His hands shook as he placed the assortment of flowers, herbs and other unusual ingredients into his large pot.

Staring wistfully into the cauldron, as the magical brew began to take shape, he couldn't help but feel the crushing weight of responsibility upon his broad shoulders. The soul of Hallowed Brook, the life of the land surrounding it, the future of its inhabitants, it all rested in his large, aged hands. And, though he was determined to do everything in his power to protect their home, the pressure upon him was palpable. He was floored by exhaustion; trying to fight against its clamouring grip.

With years of experience coursing through his giant body, years of intuition making the hairs across his huge frame stand to attention, he continued his work. There was a hush, a hush filled with a desperate hope, a deep desire that his efforts would be enough to stem the tide of disaster. Not just for the valley, not just for Hallowed Brook. This darkness had the potential to threaten everything, everyone, every creature across the whole of the planet.

"Should I be contacting Longford Grimes somehow?" He said the words aloud without realising. They slipped from between his lips and danced in the air, mixing with the mass of ingredients inside steaming the pot.

Coiling in the fragrant smelling, swirling concoction of herbs, precious crystals, and repeated incantations, he saw something emerge. A figure. A clear shape rising from the smoke. Titus Cariad felt a swift and sudden vibration pound through his Visitotem. A thrum. A powerful, unmistakable message from the spirits. He watched the curious figure rise. Was it a demon? A flamelike twist, stretch and undulation. It was as if the very core of the earth resonated, pulsed with his intentions, as if the spirits finally acknowledged the importance, saw how vital his task was, to clear the polluted air and face the evil head on. To dispel the menace that plagued them . To the giant, it was as if the realm above had finally awoken from an unnatural slumber.

The vibrations were not just physical now but seemed to reverberate through his entire being, his very soul, like a harmonious melody of guidance and encouragement.

The flame figure grew larger, pulsating in the heady steam. The spirits, in their cryptic language, were telling him that he was on the right path, that his efforts were not in vain. That they could see his overwhelming need to save his part of Celestia from certain doom. They acknowledged the threat. He watched the dancing figure within the steam once more, it shook, swirled and swelled before drifting up, up, out of the roof's opening then into the night. An elemental part of him, buoyed by his heavenly links, reached out into the ether.

Titus breathed deeply, he focused his energy on the essence of the healing mixture, infusing it with the power of his belief, his fervour in the higher realm. The Visitotem's vibrations intensified, a tremble and shake like the very earth was about to crack open. He heard a mournful rumble. Then, a hum pierced the air, the notes creating a symphony of magic that danced around him like a glittering, stretching ribbon making his starry robes sway and billow. The shape shifting figure appeared again, wrapping its arms around him, filling him with a strength that wove through his entirety. An embrace that felt unique, all consuming, before a high-pitched blast of energy took it directly upwards once again.

As the potion bubbled the vibrations gradually subsided, leaving Titus with a deep sense of calm, of order, of rebirth. The message had been clear: he had the support of the spirits in his mission to cleanse the air and protect the Brook from the threat of poisonous pollution. He also had been given a message about Eliza. Finally. It was time.

He thought about his home. The place was too precious to allow the scourge of toxicity, the meddling malice of evil, to blight it.

With the priceless potion now ready, he cradled it lovingly in his huge hands, the emerald liquid glowed in an ornate, glass bottle. As the weight of the bottle sat in his large, wrinkled palms, he once again felt his gut roil with doubt. Despite the guidance of those above, the enormous responsibility of the land's health, mixed with his ancient beliefs, his fervent hope, made him shudder and close his eyes. Titus knew deep within his bones that the fate of Hallowed Brook, the lands of the lower realm, rested upon his giant shoulders.

Looking towards Ryoni, his brow furrowed as he once again considered the connection between Ryoni's sickness, the spreading pollution and the woman, Eliza Calete. Suspicion lingered like a malevolent shadow, watching over his thoughts, noting his every move, raising questions that needed answers. He had a nagging feeling about her involvement in this, how her cold evil was tangled into the grim mess, but the true extent of her involvement remained elusive, frustratingly unclear.

Turning to his Visitotem, Titus attempted to seek guidance from the spirits once more, hoping for clarity, for coherence in his thoughts. However, his efforts were met with frustration as the same malicious, obsidian-black snake seemed to twist and coil around his link to the other realm. Her doing? Again, the presence was obstructing his attempts to delve deeper into the truth. It was as if an invisible barrier had been erected, preventing him from finding the knowledge he sought. A shadowy enchantment.

Ryoni whined low and guttural.

He couldn't get answers about Eliza. A sense of unease settled in his chest, and he realised that his powers might indeed be diminishing. He wondered again if he may be at the end of his time. The once-reliable conductor, the channel to the spiritual plane now felt tenuous, faltering in the face of this sinister force. His Visitotem no longer felt like a magical bridge between the earthly realm and the place of the spirits. It had always been so reliable, so attuned to the messages from the realm above. Now it was faltering, not always giving him anything.

"What is happening?" he muttered to himself, his voice laced with a mixture of confusion and concern. The Visitotem, once a conduit for divine insights, now felt like a dormant relic in his grasp. Merely a tall, ornate piece of wood. Doubt crept in, leaving him grappling with a sinking sense of fallibility.

Titus knew that he couldn't let this malign evil stop him. He couldn't afford to be consumed by frustration or uncertainty. This would mean that a foul force had triumphed over the elements. With a sigh, a shake of his boulder-like head, he focused his thoughts on the task at hand, clearing the polluted air and protecting his valley. The power of the spirits might be weak, but he had it. He'd been shown a chink of victory. His focus remained strong. He was sure that he could find a way to overcome these challenges, to safeguard Hallowed Brook and its people from the looming threat of pollution.

He would stop at nothing. Whatever it took, he would use everything within his power.

He sent a message out, via a Croak bird, to the other Visionaries in the nearby communities.

He hoped that other giants would heed his words of warning. Perhaps they would join together?

Regardless of Ryoni's weakened state, he needed to head up into The Desire Mountains.

What he knew about Eliza had to see the cold light of day.

He had to expose the buried darkness.

CHAPTER 25

BLUE

Blue's journey to Lumina Lake was far from easy. Each and every step was a struggle; the rugged terrain beneath her feet sent jolts of pain shooting up her spine. She gritted her teeth against the discomfort, determined not to show it, or to let the pain get the better of her. This was important, vital. As she moved forward, she couldn't help but notice how far behind she was compared to Troy and Ky, their voices carried back to her, tinkling on the breeze, as they chatted cheerfully up ahead. She shivered; the vastness of the landscape added to her sense of isolation. The wide-open space stretched before her and she willed herself to carry on.

The air around her was becoming thick with the ever-present brown ribbons of pollution, a rancid haze that made each breath feel like an effort. To Blue, every inhalation seemed to bring with it a sense of grit, a toxic heaviness, and she found herself stopping frequently to catch her breath. Her head seemed woozy, and her skin felt coated in a sandy, sticky film. Blue's determination remained fierce, but her body was fighting back. Her neck throbbed. The back pain, and the caustic air made the journey a gruelling ordeal, one that severely tested her strength and resilience.

One foot in front of the other.

Despite the physical challenges, the unsettling fog of chemicals, the bile burning her stomach, Blue pressed on. The thought of Jessie and the clues that could await them kept her going. With every step, she reminded herself of her friend's courage and bravery, her inspiring sense of adventure, she drew strength from the bond they shared. Blue was determined to uncover the truth and find Jessie, no matter what obstacles lay ahead. She had to know what had happened to her best friend.

I'm coming for you Jessie.

As they finally reached the shores of Lumina Lake, the friends paused to take in the sight before them. Despite the wisps of brown in the tainted sky and the brackish-green, frothy appearance of the water, the lake still held a magical, breathtaking beauty. It was simply mesmerising. Otherworldly rock formations dotted the edge of the lake, looking like slumbering dragons. Beyond the ledge of the lake, they could see the whole valley below them, miles and miles of natural, wide-open space. To Blue's relief, they sat for a moment, letting the tranquillity of their land wash over them. Luna, the Lunafi, was nestled between them, her amber eyes gleaming with curiosity as she too gazed around.

"Watch her a while Blue," Troy said gently. "Rest."

With a sigh, Blue stroked Luna's soft fur, finding solace in her presence. Ky and Troy set off to scour the shoreline, trying to spot anything out of the ordinary. As her fingers gently brushed over the Lunafi's silvery purple coat, her eyes settled upon something unusual, it was high up on a craggy protrusion of rock, to the right of the lake. At first, she was certain that it was a trick of the light, but as her eyes focused, she realised that it was something wrapped in a torn piece of fabric. It looked like fabric was knotted around a lump of something. As she gazed, a sinking feeling settled in Blue's stomach. A feeling of alarm. She called out to Ky and Troy, her voice carrying a mixture of urgency, fear and hope.

"Hey, you two! Come over here, quick!" Blue's voice danced across the water of the lake, drawing Ky and Troy's attention. After clambering awkwardly up on a ledge, she climbed to retrieve the rock, her fingers trembling. Her back yelling.

"Hey, be careful Blue. You could fall. What is it? What have you seen?" It was Troy.

As they joined her, helping her down. Blue held up the fabric-wrapped rock, her heart thudding and her breath raspy. "Look at this. It's a piece of Jessie's dress... tied to this piece of stone." She met their gazes, a mixture of excitement and worry clear in her eyes. It was something at least, but what the significance of it was escaped her.

"Jessie, Jessie," she called.

She turned to the men with her eyes flashing, her pain momentarily forgotten.

"Do you think she was here? Maybe she left this as a sign or a clue for us? Or do you think she could have been injured by someone?" Blue felt her knees go weak as they huddled close together, their backs against the wind, to examine the rock. Her churning mind grappled with possibilities. What were the implications of this discovery?

Blue continued to call out Jessie's name, Ky and Troy joining in, their mingled voices carrying over the rugged landscape.

"Jess, Jessie where are you? Jess it's us. It's Blue, Ky and Troy." They trudged in anxious circles, scanning the area for any signs or clues that might lead them to her. For a while, it seemed like their efforts were in vain, and frustration began to creep in. Frustration and cold. The Devout Drolle's urgent cries above added to their unease, its presence like an omen. Surely, they had to find something else.

Suddenly, Luna the Lunafi wriggled free from Troy's makeshift carrier and darted towards a crevice in the rock. Blue was startled. The friends watched in surprise as the small creature squeezed through the narrow opening. Ky's curiosity got the better of him, and Blue watched as he followed suit, managing to squeeze through the crevice after Luna. It must be bigger than it looked.

After a short while, his voice carried back to Blue and Troy, filled with a mixture of astonishment and disbelief. Blue could hear the echoing as he spoke.

"Guys, you won't believe this," Ky's voice floated back to them. "You have to see this for yourselves, it's unreal. Truly unreal." The rumble suggested he was inside a cave, the muffled noise bouncing off its walls. Blue and Troy exchanged puzzled glances before hurrying to join Ky on the other side. As they made their way through the crevice, they were greeted by an astonishing sight. Drawings and words etched into the rock surrounded them, a visual feast of creativity and a twisting dance of poignant words. Blue's heart swelled as she saw the familiar sketches before she exchanged a knowing look with Troy. Each drawing, painstakingly etched onto the rock, made her heart soar. This was incredible.

"It's Jessie's work," Blue breathed, her voice filled with awe and excitement. "She must have been here... leaving her mark, hoping we'd find it." The realisation stunned them all, a surge of clarity driving away any lingering doubts. With their friend's presence scratched clearly into the very rock of these caves, she felt an urgent sense of purpose. Despite the bitter cold, despite her raging pain, despite the anxiety gnawing at her guts. She knew now that they were on the right track, following the path that Jess had left for them and, with that driving them, they would have to keep searching, no matter where it might lead.

In caves of darkness, dreams ignite,
Whispered hope takes on flight.
Among the stones, my tale lives on,
A twisted epitaph when I'm gone.

Blue read the words aloud, the final line catching in her throat as her aquamarine eyes filled with weeks of tears. Troy's strong arms wrapped around Blue as she finally let her emotions pour forth. She couldn't contain it. Her tears mixed with the grit of the polluted air, and her wracking sobs echoed around the rocky chamber. She was consumed by a mixture of grief, fear, and a deep sense of loss. Loss of her friend. In that vulnerable moment, Troy held her close, his own face clouded with grief. He whispered comforting words, his voice a soothing balm against her piercing pain.

"Shhh... hey...I'm here for you, Blue. We're going to find her, I promise. And whatever happens, always know that I love you."

Blue's heart stalled. She shivered as the weight of Troy's declaration sank in. Her brain grappled with the three little words.

I love you.

Well, she wasn't expecting that.

These were words that she had never believed he would utter. Her heart was warmed by the revelation yet doubts and fears lingered in the back of her mind. She remembered the stories about Troy's family, the ominous presence of his aunt Eliza, and the secrets that seemed to shroud them. She remembered Jessie's terse warning. Blue looked into his eyes, searching for any trace of deception, trying to reconcile her feelings with the uncertainty that remained. Could she trust him completely? The conflict within her only deepened as she spotted a drawing of barrels with the Calete company stamp etched into the stone. His family business. A memory stirred within her.

Blue's voice wavered; her emotions palpable as she uttered her fear.

"Was this place her tomb?" The whispered words filled the air with a chilling unease. They jarred with the earlier words of devotion. Troy kissed her forehead, his fingers tracing patterns down her spine. He desperately tried to console her. Or was he distracting her from the words scratched upon the rough-hewn walls?

"Hey, you guys, get a room. Not here hey?" Ky quipped with a grin. His light-hearted comment pierced through the heaviness, injecting a touch of much-needed humour into the solemn atmosphere. The laughter served as a reminder of their bond and the strength of their friendship. Blue tried to chase away her dark worries.

Amidst the stone drawings that held Jessie's presence, their link to each other remained unbroken.

Luna, the playful creature danced around their ankles making strange whistling noises.

"So, what's the plan?" Blue asked. She wrapped her arms around herself, stepping back from Troy.

"We figure out what these drawings mean," Troy replied.

"And what the hell these creepy damned figures are too," Ky muttered, pointing at Jessie's scratched likeness of a Droid.

"I know exactly what they are," Blue muttered looking aghast. I've seen them before.

CHAPTER 26

TROY

Troy stood frozen; his eyes locked onto the single word etched onto the rock face: Calete. The weight of that name, his family name, bore down on him like a boulder, needling into the depths of his consciousness. He felt a chill crawl up his spine, a prickling of unease that threatened to burst forth from his throat as a shriek. The tender moment with Blue was now totally forgotten. Vanished.

Every fibre of his being screamed at him to run, to flee from the truth that was staring him right in the face, but he couldn't tear his eyes away. This was a confirmation.

As his mind raced, memories flooded his brain, a deluge, a torrential downpour. The barrels he had heard his aunt Eliza ordering Jessie to collect a few months back, after her and Blue had taken the supply truck to the Capital Core. The explanation he had been given was that they contained a new, natural fertiliser to help the land flourish. That it was a way to improve the growth of much needed veggies.

He gulped, a large lump of choking turmoil in his throat.

The shards of the mystery were slowly peeking out of the dirt, coming together with a clarity that sent a shiver through him. It was like a lightbulb flashing brightly in his mind. A kaleidoscope of swirling images settling to form a bright, clear picture of the truth. Those barrels weren't filled with fertiliser; they were filled with toxic dirt, a poison that was seeping into the land and corrupting the very essence of Celestia. The Capital Core's waste being dumped in their valley, in his home.

And he had stood by and let Eliza sanction it.

His gaze shifted then to Blue, who was standing beside him, her expression mirroring his own shock and disbelief. He turned to her, his voice trembling as he found the words to ask the question that hung in the air like a toxic cloud.

"You said you know what those things are...the shapes she's drawn."

"Yes, they're used in the Capital Core. They're mainly rubbish collectors. Droids that deal with waste. Dangerous chemicals I think...Haven't you ever come across them there?"

Troy thought about her words carefully. If he had he hadn't registered them as significant. He hadn't paid them any attention.

"I'm not sure, maybe...but I can't say I remember. Eliza does most of the negotiating down in The Capital. I'm always in the fields, as you know. I rarely leave my post in Elysium Meadow. But Blue, what did Jess discover about those barrels you two collected? Were the Droids connected to that?"

Blue's eyes widened in realisation, and her hand instinctively went to her mouth. "Oh no," she whispered, the weight of understanding pressing down on her.

"Those barrels... the Droids loaded them up...Jess

must have found out the truth. She had to have figured out what was inside them. It was something bad right? It has to be. I remember now...she had sketched the building in her scrapbook. It must be significant. And the faces I saw, they must have been the Droids."

"The Droids loaded up the barrels?"

Troy's heart pounded against his ribcage, a cacophony of anxiety. He paused, taking it in, trying to figure out how it all fitted together. A myriad of emotions made him dizzy. Anger, betrayal, fear. A jittery feeling unsteadied him, everything that he felt he knew was widening like a chasm beneath him, falling away.

Unable to look any longer, he turned away from the etchings on the rock, his mind reeling as he reflected on Jessie's discoveries. He had been living in ignorance, oblivious to the sinister plots that had been unfolding right under his nose. His aunt, Eliza Calete, with her darkness, must be involved in this toxic deception, and he couldn't help but feel a surge of disgust and fury.

"The barrels Blue, what had Jess discovered about those barrels you two collected?" he asked Blue again, his voice a mixture of urgency and desperation.

Blue's voice trembled.

"I don't know what Jess had uncovered...but... she's clever, inquisitive, she must have realised something. I can't remember what she wrote in her scrapbook when she sketched that warehouse we went to. You think she stumbled across something she shouldn't have right?"

"She did. She must have. I think I know now what was in those barrels." He looked down to the floor. "I think it's to do with the pollution, the Brook, the poisoning of the land. The diseased animals."

"So, what? Are you saying Eliza was bringing toxic waste from the capital to the Brook? That's what this is about? Hell, Jess must have found out. Tell me. Do you think that's what this is all about Troy?" Blue said, her eyes brimming with tears. "Did you know? Have you been hiding this? Jessie would have known what was happening here, exactly what your aunt Eliza was doing. Did you know?"

The reality hit him like a punch to the gut. His family was responsible for this devastation, this corruption of their home. His aunt, the one he had once blindly trusted, had betrayed them all. Jess had been taken by forces connected to this sinister secret. Anguish welled up within him, threatening to consume him whole. He clenched his fists, hard. Troy's knuckles became white, his back taut, his chestnut eyes damp, overcome with the gravity of his emotions.

"I didn't know. I swear. I know that there were shady deals... links to Longford Grimes but... no. There's something else. Another secret... that's what I thought this was about. Not pollution. Not poisoned dirt. We have to find Jessie now," Troy declared, his voice firm. "We have to uncover the full extent of what's happening, exactly what's going on and then maybe we can find a way to put an end to it."

Blue nodded, her eyes lingering on his face, trying to read him, to see if she could trust him. Could she trust him?

The rest would have to wait. The other dark truths, the secrets and lies.

"This is Jessie. No matter what we need to bring her home. We've got to. I think we can, Troy. We'll find Jess and we'll expose the truth no matter how hard that may be. But hear me out, we really need to be careful, to plan our next move. Your aunt..."

Troy took a deep breath, he knew exactly what she was trying to say, his mind racing with the weight of responsibility that now rested upon his young shoulders. Part of the truth had been revealed, and there was no turning back.

"Jess wrote about her didn't she? She wrote about my aunt in her sketchbooks. That's why you didn't want me to tell her about the trip up here."

"Yes... nothing definite. Nothing clear. But she wrote her name, many times toward the end of the book and each time it was shaded in dark strokes. I saw some words too about Eliza Calete being a toxic force."

He stared at a word on the rock TOXIC. It blared like a continuous alarm. His eyes returned to Blue; his gaze unwavering. "We'll discuss my aunt in good time. For now, Jessie is the priority. We'll do whatever it takes to save Jessie then stop this toxic deception. I have things to reveal, things that have been pulling me down, burying me. Let's make a plan and talk. Just promise me that we'll face it together."

They stood there then, surrounded by the etchings, knowing instinctively that what lay ahead was perilous. Dirt had been revealed, and more dirt would follow. Troy was ready to face whatever stood in their way, in order to end this. Despite it being hazardous, despite it being fraught with complications, despite it being a fight they may never win.

He was prepared to cut ties with his family to try to

undo some of the harm carried out under the Calete name.

And, he knew that he had something he needed to reveal before they went any further. Somehow though, the words refused to form.

Like a spell had been cast, making him silent.

CHAPTER 27

JESS

She had suspected it before, but this confirmed it. Yes. She had finally pieced it all together. She was certain now. Eliza Calete had made her collect toxic waste, waste that was destroying the area, waste that was poisoning the land. She'd been used in a plot to destroy the very place she adored. It stung. Heat burned in her chest. But, at last she had a reason for her gut feeling. The feeling that Eliza Calete was somehow a dark, toxic figure who needed to be approached with caution. The things she had seen, they now made sense.

The memories of that fateful day flooded her mind, and she felt a knot of anxiety tightening in her stomach. She knew now, without a shadow of a doubt, that the woman who had questioned her was definitely Eliza Calete. The final pieces of this conundrum were falling into place, revealing a disturbing truth that Jessie just couldn't ignore. There was a malevolence in Eliza, an evil that she had tried to bury before, but she was willingly showing now. There could be no going back.

The presence of the Droids disturbed her. Behind her eyelids she could see their unnatural forms. Their red laser eyes, the eerie way they moved, their mechanical voices. Being around them, it sent shivers down her spine. They were always watching.

She thought back then, to seeing the droids working. They were looking at footage of people on screens, listening to people too...ordinary people. There had been graphs on some of those screens too...representations of the decline of different Celestia species. It had chilled her.

She remembered the first time she had ever seen a Droid. It was that same day that she had picked up the barrels. She had been ordered to collect them, transport them back to Hallowed Brook, then deliver them to a designated meeting place. All the while she was completely unaware of the sinister purpose behind the innocent task. She was just an employee following orders. Collecting, transporting delivering.

She had no clue that what she was doing would cause all this harm.

She had approached the warehouse, seen the Droids, watched as they loaded up. Watched their other odd behaviours...how they had stared at those screens. All the while Blue had sat in the company truck, her head stuck firmly in a book as per usual, totally oblivious.

The memory rang strident. Like a blaring siren. Eliza telling Jess that she had to collect barrels of a special, natural fertiliser. Her smiling face as she talked about how important it was. How it was a breakthrough for the company. It had all been a cover, a damned smokescreen, fabricated to hide the dangerous truth. And, those Droids had been spying on Celestians. She felt it in her guts.

Jessie's mind raced, circling back to the barrels she had seen after that day, the ones littering the shore of Lumina Lake. Discarded, left behind, like a dirty trail of pebbles leading to a filthy secret. Breadcrumbs of Eliza's

DIRT

barbarity. She had noticed the labels, the strange odours emanating from them, but at the time, she had brushed it off as inconsequential.

How wrong she had been.

Now, the image was becoming clearer, the hidden parts illuminated, painting a horrifying picture of what was happening in the shadows. Right in the heart of the Calete company, in the Elysium Fields, within Hallowed Brook and here at Lumina Lake. Jessie had known the land was becoming polluted, but little did she know that she'd had a direct hand in causing it. Guilt swarmed around her like stinging insects.

Where else had Eliza poisoned?

The Devout Drolle's haunting calls echoed shrilly in her ears. It was as if the majestic creature was trying to communicate, trying to pass on a message, a message that Jess was struggling to decipher.

She looked up. Could the Devout Drolle somehow sense her distress, her desperation for answers? It seemed far-fetched, but in this surreal world she now found herself ensnared in, anything was possible.

Emotionally drained, she slumped onto the cold floor, her mind raced with thoughts of her friends. Of Blue, Troy, and Ky. She clung to the memories of their laughter, their time spent gazing at stars, the jokes in the fields and the unspoken ties that bound them.

Did Troy know?

Blue was the reason she hadn't given up, the reason she had fought against the darkness that threatened to consume her. It was Blue's friendship that had sustained her. She ached to see Blue. Her friend's face danced vividly

169

behind her eyelids.

The weight of the grim situation pressed down heavily on Jessie's shoulders, pushing her lower and lower. She knew for a fact that she couldn't stay confined in this cave forever. She had to find a way out, to completely uncover the truth, and she had to stop whatever treacherous plans were being put into motion by that damned witch of a woman. More pollution. More destruction. More death. It simply couldn't happen. Eliza Calete had to pay for what she had done. The sketches she had left on the walls, they could tell the story even if she couldn't. But she wanted to tell it herself. Speak her truth. She had to.

As she closed her eyes again, Jessie felt a choking mixture of despair, doubt and devastation, it poisoned her bloodstream, coursing through her veins. Like their poisoned Brook.

The Devout Drolle's call grew louder, almost as if it were urging her to persevere, to find a way. She clung to a sliver of hope, a small sliver that was disappearing rapidly like melting ice.

With a deep breath, she paused to allow herself to think of a plan, her mind twisting and turning with countless questions.

"I need to get out!"

Jessie's mind whirled as she considered the Droids that had captured her. She remembered the unnerving sight of their red laser eyes, like predatory creatures locked onto their prey. Their movements were calculated, precise, and utterly inhuman. The way they had spoken to her, their voices usually completely devoid of emotion, sent a chill down her spine. There was no doubt in her mind that, like the Droids at the Capital Core warehouse, these Droids were under someone's command, and that someone surely had to be Eliza Calete. Eliza was using these Droids, these mechanical enforcers, to carry out her sinister plots. Plots that involved the toxic barrels, the pollution of their land, and the change that had occurred at Lumina Lake. They were acting kind now, before the hammer blow fell. Tricking her. She was on to them.

Jess couldn't shake the feeling that she was just an insignificant problem in a much more complex, shady plot. Insignificant and disposable. That would be exactly what they would do. Dispose of her. This was a shady scheme that threatened not only her life but the very fabric of Celestia itself.

The Droids' presence, back before she had been captured, back in the warehouse, surrounded by barrels of toxic waste, back before the lake had been tainted, was a chilling image burned into her memory. Their role in this operation was clear. The unfeeling machines, the unquestioning machines, the unconcerned enforcers of Eliza's dark agenda. And now, as Jess sat in the cold cave, she understood the gravity of the situation. Eliza's actions weren't just harming the environment; they were endangering the lives of every living being on their planet. Beyond Hallowed Brook, beyond The Desire Mountains. This dirt would infiltrate every corner of their land unless she was brought to justice.

The Devout Drolle's calls seemed to underscore the urgency of the situation. Jess had a feeling that the huge, majestic creature could sense the impending danger, the looming catastrophe that Eliza's actions were creating. The Drolle's plaintive cries were a haunting reminder that time was now of the essence, that she couldn't afford to waste a single moment in exposing the truth, that she needed to stop ruminating and find a way to act.

She knew that she had to find a way to escape this cave, to reveal Eliza's true intentions, and to protect the planet she loved. Her earlier scratches and sketches, the ones she had left on the first cave's walls, had showed her facing up to her fears, expressing all that had become clear after months in darkness. She had scratched the small snippets of the picture until they had become a clear image. Those scratched marks were a silent cry for help and justice. But, on those walls, there was a part missing, the crux of the story. With each scratch of her makeshift tools, she had channelled her frustration, her anger, and her hope. But she had lacked a key part of the riddle.

The truth was now clear: Eliza Calete was a threat, and Jessie was determined to expose her. With the image of the Droids and the barrels imprinted on her mind, she vowed to uncover the truth, to get back to the Brook, back to her friends, back to work. Her work now would be putting an end to the pollution and destruction that had begun to mar their world. She knew that the fight she faced wouldn't be easy.

Jessie's eyes darted around the cave; her thoughts consumed by the need for escape. The cold, hard stone walls seemed to taunt her, determined to hold her captive, to trap her in the grim prison. But then, as her gaze swept over the rocky nooks and crannies, she spotted something that ignited a spark of hope within her.

DIRT

There, in a corner of the cave, was a narrow crevice. Faint light, from the outside poured through. This was a sliver of an opening, a split in the rock that led to the unknown. It was small, barely wide enough for her to squeeze through, but it offered a glimmer of possibility. Jess's heart pounded as she crawled over to the crack in the rock, her fingers brushed against the rough edges.

Carefully, she peered inside, the darkness within shrouding the crevices destination. It was a risk, but it was a chance she was willing to take. With legs trembling, with her head swirling, Jess began to wriggle her way into the narrow passage, her body contorting, squeezing to fit the tight space.

The crevice was claustrophobic, the earth pressing in on all sides as she wormed her way forward. She gulped. Panic threatened to overtake her, but she fought to stay calm, focusing on the end goal of freedom. Freedom for her and for Celestia. The minutes stretched on, each inch gained felt like an eternity, but Jess pressed onward still, driven by the desperation to escape her captors and bring the truth to light. She was dizzy, finding it hard to breathe and blackness danced in the corners of her vision. Sweat stung her eyes. Her muscles screeched.

Finally, after one last exhausting shimmy, Jess emerged from the crevice into a dimly lit chamber. The air was damp and musty, the cavern was pierced by thin shards of light from holes up above. Looking around, she shivered. Her heart pounded with a mixture of relief and anxiety. She had escaped the confines of the cave, but this was far from over.

As she stood in the chamber, Jess's mind sifted

through her options. She needed to find a way back to Hallowed Brook, to her friends, and to the answers that could expose Eliza Calete's sinister plans.

The Devout Drolle's cries echoed in her memory, a reminder of how urgent this was. With steely determination, Jess took a deep breath and began to explore her surroundings, ready to squeeze through more tunnels to get out. To clamber through whatever blocked the path to truth and justice.

But there was a problem. Before she'd had some sense of the cave system, openings and tunnels. She'd had a rough map in her head that she'd etched on the wall. But the more they'd moved her, the more disorientated she'd become. Where the hell was she now?

CHAPTER 28

THE VISIONARY

Titus Cariad stood at the edge of the rocky outcrop; his eyes fixed on the smog-choked sky that now hung over Hallowed Brook like a blanket of foreboding. The once pristine air had been tainted again, and he could feel the weight of the pollution pressing against his chest. It was as if the very land itself was crying out for help, and he knew that he had to do something more.

He had used the potion, allowing the fumes to drift into the atmosphere. It had temporarily caused the air to clear, for the blue of the sky to fight against the grime. For a few hours it had seemed like he had succeeded. But he was now back to square one. The magic had failed.

Turning his attention back to the polluted sky, Titus closed his eyes and reached out with his mind, seeking the connection to the spirits. But once again, he was met with resistance, a black, coiling barrier that blocked him from accessing the guidance, the visions that had always been his source of power. Frustration welled within him, and he clenched his fists in anger. He hardly ever got angry, hardly ever got mad, but things were rapidly spiralling out of his control.

Ryoni whined softly, his amber eyes lacked the light

that usually flared like a beacon. Titus knelt beside the wolf, his large hand continually stroking the wolf's fur.

"We'll find a way to put all of this right Ryoni. I promise. We must. I think we need to venture up, to visit Lumina Lake.

As the sun dipped below the horizon, casting a golden hue across the polluted sky, Titus Cariad's thoughts turned to Ky, Blue, and Troy. They were on their own journey, seeking answers about Jessie's disappearance. Trying to unravel the mystery of where she may be. He knew that their quest was essential, but he also felt a growing sense of agitation, portentous thoughts plagued him. There was an undeniable connection between the pollution, the Droids, and Eliza Calete, and Titus couldn't shake the feeling that time may be running out. There was something else too. A sense that there was something or someone they had overlooked.

With a solemn sigh, Titus rose to his feet and turned his attention to his hut. He needed to gather some supplies and make his way up to Lumina Lake. He couldn't stand idly by while his land suffered, while his villagers faced danger, and while the light of truth remained buried in darkness.

He summoned his weary Shadow Wolf. The upward journey from his rocky abode was focused and quick, the sense of urgency reverberating in his heavy steps. Ryoni managed to keep up, his body pointing forward but his tail down.

As Titus arrived, he noticed distressed expressions upon the faces of the birds, and other woodland creatures that he passed. They, too, were feeling the effects of the pollution, and the fear of the unknown seemed to be weighing heavily upon them. Their sixth sense was making them skittish, fretful. It was as if the Desire Mountains had become a place of wariness instead of wonder.

By the lake, Titus found himself approaching familiar faces: Ky, Blue, and Troy. Their ashen expressions told a story of their own worries and discoveries.

"Tell me, what has happened. What have you found?"

"Yes, you need to know Titus. Just let us gather our thoughts. We've had quite a day. We have discovered something significant," Blue replied, her eyes red rimmed.

As he sat by the discoloured water, Ryoni settled close by his side. His golden furred wolf was still not back to his usual form, but his jittery gait had improved.

Titus noticed that Ky's jovial demeanour was absent, replaced by a seriousness that mirrored the gravity of the situation. Blue's drawn expression spoke of her concern for Jess and her own struggles with physical pain. And Troy, his troubled gaze revealed the burden of his family's secrets and the knowledge he now carried. He looked like he was wrestling with the truth he'd not shared. Titus would have to press him.

"We've found a cave," Blue began, her voice steady despite the emotions that lay beneath the surface.

"There're signs. Scratched drawings that Jessie has made on the walls. They're crucial, very crucial."

As he listened intently, she recounted their journey to Lumina Lake, the torn fabric tied around the stone, and the cave. Finally, she explained what they had seen, the story told by the sketches etched into the rocks.

"She'd drawn barrels, barrels from Calete Company.

Barrels that we collected from the Capital Core."

Titus looked at Troy. As Blue spoke, The Visionary's mind raced. The pieces were coming together, forming a picture of Eliza Calete's involvement in the pollution of the valley and the potential long-term threat it posed to the health of their land.

"And these drawings, you're sure they're Jessie's?" Titus asked, his voice tinged with urgency.

" Yes! They are a warning, a message. Jess knew something. I'd show you, but you'd never fit through. The cave itself is too cramped."

Titus nodded; his mind worked to connect the dots. "Eliza Calete's involvement does seem clear. I believe she's behind this pollution, and it seems she's been using the Droids to carry out her sinister plans." Troy, eyes grim, looked to the ground awkwardly. There was more to reveal.

Ky leaned forward; his eyes fixed on Titus. "We need to confront her, expose her. But we also need to find Jessie. I don't want to put Jess in any further danger. Eliza has to be challenged, but not before we have a sure way to save Jessie first."

The warning in Ky's words mirrored Titus' own thoughts. They were facing a two-fold challenge. They needed to uncover the exact truth behind the pollution and locate their missing friend safely. The two tasks were undoubtedly intertwined, and Titus knew that their actions needed to be considered, they would no doubt impact the future of Celestia. And, of course, there was the secret hovering in the air unsaid.

"Troy, I think it's time to tell them what you know. I

know it's difficult but it's vital. We all need to know Eliza's true character. What we are dealing with."

Troy looked around, his eyes flicking from face to face, he looked down at the ground then up at Titus. His chestnut eyes revealed that he too wanted to unburden himself, make the truth known.

"Yes, it's time," Troy murmured.

CHAPTER 29

BLUE

Blue stared at the man she had shared so many moments with. Such intimate moments. Her anger flared and she felt the ground spin. She had shared so much of herself with a liar.

Closing her eyes against the hurt, she listened to the dark truth. She couldn't believe what was coming out of his mouth.

"My aunt Eliza is a sorceress. She has been causing dark, dangerous things to happen in the Brook for years. Before my time even. I only found out recently and … well…she threatened to harm my father if I spoke out. She's hidden him away, taken him somewhere…he's very sick."

"What the hell Troy? A sorceress…but…that's insane," Blue struggled to comprehend the words that tripped off his tongue. They left his lips like they were the most natural things in the world to say. She was dumbstruck, reeling.

"I went to Titus for advice…as soon as I was completely sure… I told him some of the things I'd found…not everything though." The words were twisting and turning like a storm. Blue stared, her mouth agape and her pulse pounding in her ears.

Blue's heart was a tempestuous sea, her emotions crashing like waves against the shore as she absorbed the full force of Troy's revelation. This man, the man she thought she loved, had been hiding unfathomable secrets. Fury simmered beneath the surface, a burning ember of flickering flame amidst the turbulent whirls of confusion.

Standing by the murky waters of Lumina Lake, she felt a surge of frustration. Troy had kept this from her, from them, for so long. Her eyes, once warm and trusting, now dimmed with the tinge of betrayal.

"We're your friends though. Why would you keep it hidden Troy?" Her voice was edged with the sharpness of her emotions. "Why did you keep this from me, from us?" She tossed her long, brown locks over her shoulder. She knew she was repeating herself, saying the same words over and over, but she couldn't help it.

Troy's gaze fell to the polluted lake, his own frustration flashing in his chestnut eyes.

"Blue, I was afraid, scared of her threats and I didn't know how to tell you. I didn't want to burden you with the darkness that surrounds my family, with what Eliza has done. It's all so... complicated. I don't think I fully know the extent of how she has used her magic, and how she's meddled in other things…man-made dangers as well as spells."

She couldn't quite get a handle on exactly what he was saying, it all sounded garbled, like she was listening underwater. Ky seemed to take the news a little less emotionally, his blonde head bowed, listening. He moved in close and placed a hand on Blue's shoulder, his voice steady, calming and his amber eyes serious. His usual humour completely absent.

"Hey, I get it. I understand that this isn't easy, Blue. But it doesn't seem to me like Troy has had it easy either. Troy's been carrying this weight alone, dealing with his father's illness too. As well as the fear of what his crazy Aunt Eliza might do. I guess he may have needed time to get his head around it all. To be sure. At least he's telling us now…right?"

Blue's incendiary anger began to cool, replaced by a reluctant sense of acceptance. She knew Troy well enough to recognise that he wasn't keeping secrets to hurt them. He was clearly grappling with his own fears and long buried uncertainties.

"Guys, I'm so sorry," he mouthed, his cheeks flushed and his voice quaking. He wrapped a brown arm across his stomach. She felt a surge of guilt then.

Troy turned towards Blue, his features pleading, the rawness evident in his voice. His chestnut eyes were sheened with unshed tears.

"I'm worried about her dark magic, the depths of her evil intentions. I didn't want any of you to be in danger because of me. Because of her. But I guess it's too late for that now. She's already hurt one of us. Jessie has been placed in danger… and… well I've been grappling with how to deal with what I've discovered in the last few months, but I'm sure now. I need to confront Eliza, for my father's sake, for Jess, and for the Brook. It's all a mess. Such a mess."

Blue sighed, her earlier confusion giving way to understanding.

. "You're right, Troy. We need to face this together,

pool our skills, our thoughts. We'll find Jess and put an end to whatever Eliza is up to, what chaos she is causing with her dark magic. But from now on, no more secrets, okay? Please." She placed her arms around him.

Troy nodded, falling into her warmth. There was a mixture of relief and gratitude in his eyes.

Titus listened intently, gazing at the three of them with a wise shimmer lighting up his moonlike face, as if he was pleased that they had resolved things without him needing to intervene. He nodded decisively and smiled. Ryoni let out a low, mournful howl and Blue patted the Shadow Wolf on his flank. The Lunafi wriggled up Troy's leg, her tail flicking and he pulled her gently into his arms.

"Hey! You crazy creature, quit it, your nails are sharp!"

"You brought that thing along buddy, you can't complain now," Ky laughed.

"She led us to the cave; she's a clever little thing aren't you, Luna?" Blue giggled scratching the silver Lunafi between her ears.

"Hey, she's here thanks to Titus. It was The Visionary who told me to find an animal in need. Hang on..." The cogs began to twist and turn in Troy's mind. Blue knew that look. "You knew..."

"Yes, it was fated Troy. Many things on Celestia are bound into the intricacies of fate. Written in Celestia's stars you might argue," the giant added.

They stood by Lumina Lake, the lapping of the polluted waters a stark reminder of the challenges ahead. With the lanterns they had lit now casting eerie reflections on the murky surface, they shared a silent pact, pledging to confront the harm that threatened the Brook and to stand together in the face of whatever mysteries The Desire Mountains held.

"There're so many more details about what I suspect Eliza and her evil magic have caused...I could be here all-night ruminating over her deeds, but the priority is Jessie right?"

"Yep, let's not get distracted by that witch. That's what she would want Troy. Instead, I think we need another look at those drawings, see if there's anything else to guide us. We need to go back into the cave and properly study everything that Jessie scratched on those walls," Blue replied, her voice steady and sure.

***

As Blue stared at the intricate drawings on the rock once again, her heart thudded, and her mind raced with a myriad of ideas. She focused on the map that Jess had sketched to the right of the words and pictures. It seemed to show the cave system. From the depicted tunnels, the whole area seemed complex and mysterious, yet this makeshift map held the promise of answers. The image of the Devout Drolle, woven into the sketches, only deepened Blue's belief that there was something they were missing. The lantern light made everything seem mystical, the images undulating and dancing. It was as if Jess had left a puzzle for them to solve.

Her mind raced as she considered the implications of the drawing of the map. If Jess had created this depiction based on the sounds she heard, it meant she might still be held within this very cave system, she could be somewhere nearby. Blue's fingers traced the lines of the sketch, her urge to find her friend growing stronger with each passing moment. She saw how the map of the tunnels stretched to the other side of the wide expanse of Lumina Lake.

The scratched likeness of the glorious Devout Drolle seemed to speak to her. Her eyes were drawn to it like a magnet. It shimmered in the candle flame.

"Hey, Troy," she began, turning to him with a spark of hope in her eyes. "Didn't you mention that your ancestors used to ride the Devout Drolles? What if we could try to do the same? Perhaps you have an innate connection to them. If you could fly on one of the Drolles, we might be able to cover a larger area and search for signs of where Jess could be. Look, this is the other side of the lake. You could fly over there. The land would look clearer from the skies."

Troy's expression shifted as he mulled over the idea. "Well…I guess I could give it a try. It's a long shot, but if it helps us find Jess, it's certainly worth attempting."

Blue's heart swelled with a deep sense of gratitude. Her love for Troy becoming stronger with his willingness to try her perilous idea. She knew that trying to tame a Devout Drolle would be incredibly risky, but the urgency of their need to find Jess before she came to further harm, had forced her to consider every possible way forward. Even ones that sounded nuts. Jessie would be pleased with her brazenness, throwing caution to the wind, literally.

But what else could they do?

Turning from the sketches, she took one last look at the images and words, then shimmied up, climbing through the crevice, the thick, jagged rock, back to Titus, Ryoni and the Lunafi. Ignoring the agony in her twisted neck and back. She smiled as she saw the tiny creature lay nestled in the giant's thick, meaty arms. Troy and Ky followed behind, blinking as they emerged onto the shores of the lake once more.

Blue turned her gaze to Titus, she buried her pain, focusing instead on her racing mind that brimmed with ideas.

"We want to see if we can get above these rocks, to get a better picture of the system of caves from the air. Troy is going to try and fly a Devout Drolle, just like his forefathers used to. Could you help us Titus? with your connection to the spirits and your understanding of the land, is there something we can do to tempt the Drolle? To tame it? We need all the support we can get."

Titus's eyes met Blue's, and she saw a hesitancy in his eyes. Then he gazed up at the brown, smoggy air that hung like thick ribbons in the sky.

"I'll do my best," he replied. "I'll commune with the spirits and see if they can offer any suggestions. The Drolle is a powerful beast, it shouldn't be underestimated."

As they continued to discuss their plan, Blue's mind raced with possibilities. The combination of Troy's family link to the Devout Drolles and Titus's connection to the spirits could provide them with the very tools that they needed to uncover Jess's whereabouts. The urgency of the situation weighed heavily on her. She found herself nibbling at her lip, staring off into space.

"I can use Ryoni to communicate with the Devout Drolles," Titus suggested, his eyes fixed on his shadow wolf. "Ryoni and I have a connection that runs deep, and the spirits often use him as a bridge for communication, communication between us."

Blue's head seemed to spin ever onwards, becoming

overwhelmed. The thought of Ryoni acting as a conduit between them and the Devout Drolles seemed to make sense if it would work.

"Hey, Titus. Remember how he behaved back in the Brook when the Drolle flew over, could that have been a sign? Giving us a clue... Damn, was that only the other day?" Ky's voice came to her as if from far away.

"Yes, you're right, I remember." She heard Titus reply.

She shook herself as if she were shaking off a layer of ice. Looking around at them all, her eyes focused and her mind clearer, she nodded, a mixture of anticipation and excitement building within her. Anything but focus on the raw pain.

"Let's do it," Troy muttered firmly. "We need every advantage we can get."

Titus stood up; his gaze fixed on the Devout Drolle soaring overhead.

"Ryoni," he called softly, and the Shadow Wolf trotted over to him, his amber eyes filled with trust and understanding. With a glance exchanged between them, Titus knelt down and whispered something deep into the wolf's ear, something that Blue couldn't hear.

Moments later, Ryoni lifted his head and emitted a series of low, melodic howls, a chilling sound. It was like a ballad, a strident response to the Devout Drolle's calls. The majestic bird circled lower, its sapphire feathers glinting in the moonlight. Blue watched with bated breath as the two creatures seemed to communicate in a language that only they could understand. A language of magical beings.

After a few moments, Titus turned to the group, amazement clear upon his face.

"The Devout Drolle knows something," he breathed. "It's leading us. We should follow... Can you manage to follow?"

The darkness was like a cloak and Blue was terrified she might fall; she clenched her jaw against the tenderness in her lower back, her whole spine seemed like a locked column of steel. They had to follow. No matter what. Every onward step grated.

With Ryoni at his side and the Devout Drolle leading the way, the group trailed behind the giant. The moonlight illuminated a path through the peaks, but she feared what lay ahead. Calling upon her inner strength, she hoped this path would be one that finally led the way to the truth.

As they followed the majestic bird through the rugged landscape, the sky began to lighten. How could it be another day? Another day without Jessie. Another day without answers. She struggled to keep positive then, her eyes heavy and her limbs weary. Blue tried to take solace in the fact that she was surrounded by friends who shared her desire to get to the bottom of this, as well as a fierce loyalty to one another. That might see them through.

They trudged on as night handed over the reins to day. As the dawn broke on the icy, bitter slopes, she took in the sights, sounds and smells of this outstanding landscape.

Up ahead, in the morning wisps of orange and purple, sat a nest. The spectacular nest of the Devout Drolle.

CHAPTER 30

TROY

As the female bird tiptoed slowly towards him, leaving its nest and approaching Troy almost as if it knew that he was always going to come here, the enormity of the creature was awe-inspiring. The male had led them here, before settling onto the nest with his squalling chicks.

He marvelled as her sapphire feathers glinted like fire in the early sunlight. The majestic poise of the elegant creature was even more pronounced this close up. Troy stood before the Drolle utterly transfixed; his feet firmly lodged in the dirt, numb. Could he possibly hope to ride upon her sleek, gigantic body? The very idea seemed completely absurd to him. Like a sure-fire way to get himself killed. He blinked his chestnut eyes in a confused flicker. The Drolle came closer still. Its eyes bored into him.

This is ludicrous.

Nevertheless, he could feel the weight pressing upon his shoulders. The quest to uncover the truth behind Jessie's disappearance, to confront the pollution that threatened their land, and to face the darkness that lingered within his family's past.

Taking a deep breath, Troy tentatively approached the vivid, breath-taking bird. He extended a trembling hand, hesitating for a moment before gently touching her head. The Devout Drolle's eyes continued to fix upon him, its gaze steady and piercing. The deep eyes were orbs in which he saw strange shapes dancing. He was sure the creature could see into his very soul, as if it was sensing his doubts and fears.

Yes, totally overwhelmed with fear.

It had been waiting, fated. Like the Lunafi. He could sense this truth deep within his twisting gut. Troy placed a hand upon the creature's neck and gingerly began to climb onto her sturdy back. His heart thrummed with alarm as he settled himself comfortably between the bird's enormous wings, his legs straddled the powerful, lithe body. It felt natural. Like coming home. A jolt of generational memories, memories from his ancestors, span like a kaleidoscope within his mind. The feathers beneath his fingers were surprisingly soft, a stark contrast to the creature's imposing size.

"Are you okay Troy?" Blue shouted from their vantage point across from the nest. They hadn't wanted to spook the creatures or their chicks.

"Kind of," he replied honestly.

As he gazed about, figuring out how to steer the damned thing, he heard a series of low, guttural cheeps, they sounded far too delicate for the bird's colossal frame. He held onto the feathers around her neck tightly, his knuckles turning white as he fought to steady his racing thoughts.

Relax. This was almost meant to be.

Then the Devout Drolle let out a high-pitched, resonating call, its sound reverberating through Troy's fluttering chest. He could feel the vibrations beneath him, a reminder of the wildness of this creature. Troy closed his chestnut eyes briefly, summoning his courage as well as summoning the spirits of his ancestors. He delved into the sands of time, of the time before. With his head down, he tried to visualise Erodan's bravery, feel the connection with these creatures that stretched back into the past, stitched and woven into the ephemeral ribbons of time. He willed the ancient connection to flow through his fingers.

As the Devout Drolle's wings began to rhythmically beat, Troy felt a jolt of raw exhilaration.

He was ready.

Everything fell away. It was as if his focus narrowed to just him, the bird and the land. He looked around at the orange-tinged breaking of day, it was a new dawning. The ground beneath him receded, and he was lifted up high into the sky. The sensation was both thrilling and terrifying. The wild rush of wind whipped around him as they gained altitude. He felt the bitterness pierce his skin as the penetrating cold cloaked him. Troy's grip on the feathers tightened instinctively, and he forced himself to relax, to trust in the bond that had existed between Caletes and the Devout Drolles generations ago. He wanted to trust his gut. Trust the bond. Trust the magic that wound between the Devout Drolle and the Caletes. He prayed this would work.

With each beat of the bird's wings, Troy's fear slowly began to ebb. With a gasp, he opened his eyes to a breathtaking view. It was like he had slipped into a higher plain, to the realm beyond. The land below twinkled like paradise. As he glanced down, the sprawling landscape of the icy Desire Mountains lay bare before him, waking from slumber. The sparkling rivers, the patchwork forests below, the eerie green of Lumina Lake and their small home nestled right in the verdant core of the valley. The Brook was still smudged with a brown smear of pollution. This sight transfixed him, it was a perspective he had never imagined. Not even in his wildest dreams could he have imagined the pure, elemental beauty. Even with the thick ropes of polluted air. It came with a visceral reminder that the outstanding richness and mesmerising vitality of their planet was at risk of being lost. Lost forever. The ruddy clouds, the colour of dirt, taunted him.

He had to stop Eliza.

As they soared even higher, Troy's focus shifted from pure amazement to the more pressing search for Jessie. He tried to clear his mind, apart from thoughts of her. He imagined Jess, recalled her drawings etched onto the rock, narrowed his mind to the clues she had left behind for them. He thought of the Devout Drolle's urgent calls and the way these fascinating creatures had a deep connection to the heart of their world. Troy felt adrenaline surging around his veins, making each and every hair on his body raise. Goosebumps marched across his skin like the wild and free Saint Blurts. He knew that they were battling against time now, that the pollution, the damage to the land, the harm to the animals here had to be stopped. It was down to them, before irreparable destruction altered the landscape of Celestia forever.

Almost instinctively, Troy guided the Devout Drolle back towards Lumina Lake, his hands trembled, but his need to act overpowered the creeping anxiety. The green-tinged polluted waters came into view, a stark reminder of the lies, secrets and plots that had already unfolded here. Of the buried dirt already scarring the land, altering the place he called home. It was already manacling and diverting the never-ending rhythm of the circle of life in this place. He knew that their quest was bigger than any one person. It was bigger than finding Jessie. Bigger than reining in the malice of his aunt. As he took a stomach somersaulting look across the wide expanse of the slowly waking Celestia, the place filled with creatures, his home that lay beneath him, the Brook, he knew that this was about saving their planet, their freedoms, and the lives of the thousands upon thousands of creatures that called this valley their own.

With a deep breath, Troy turned the bird's flight towards the rocky expanse that held the tunnels and caves, his gaze determined. He was ready to unravel the connections between the pollution, the Droids, and Jessie's strange disappearance. He was ready to face the challenges ahead, to bring the truth to light, and to restore the land that had been tainted by darkness.

As he soared forward, his resolve solidified. He was no longer alone in this fight. He had the support of his friends, the guidance of The Visionary, and the bond he shared with the Devout Drolle. With every beat of its wings, he moved ever closer to the answers he sought. He could feel it.

But he'd not anticipated the fact that Aunt Eliza was also a Calete. That her ancestors were his. That they had flown the Devout Drolle and that she too could harness its power.

The sight of her chilled him. He almost tumbled

backwards. Nearly losing his grip on the bird and plummeting through the sky.

Eliza Calete's malevolence seemed to know no bounds as she soared through the azure sky on the back of her own Devout Drolle. Another huge female.

Why hadn't he made that connection?

Her piercing eyes gleamed with malice as she cast her gaze downward, soaring above Troy. He was stunned. Blindsided. He looked up becoming dizzy, wobbling precariously on the bird's broad back. His brain began scrabbling to register the full extent of the threat.

Of course, she would use her magic and her connection.

He shivered and watched her skilfully direct the menacing bird towards him. Troy realised that his presence was a continual thorn in her side. She must know that he had uncovered more truths. He could see the determination in her green eyes, the unyielding wickedness that refused to back down, even when confronted by her nephew.

"Surprise surprise, oh Troy what a family reunion… and look…I see you have a friend with you nephew, you can also ride the Drolle. Maybe, not quite as well as me though. Isn't that right my boy?" Her words came to him, twisting through the air.

He was dumbfounded. His grip on the bird faltered as he took in her wild red hair and her caustic gaze.

"Eliza, stop this now. Please Eliza."

With a cruel smile, she urged her Drolle onward, pushing it to greater heights. He watched as Eliza's fingers traced the patterns that mottled the creature's feathers, invoking ancient incantations of power. Words began tumbling from her lips, repeated words. Over and over. She was casting a spell.

As she chanted, the sky itself seemed to respond, clouds swirling ominously around her. A light rain sprinkled them, distracting Troy.

The Devout Drolle beneath her began to dive, its wings slicing through the air like sharp blades. Eliza's maniacal laughter echoed in the heavens, a sinister melody that sent shivers down Troy's spine. Could they hear it down below on the ground? Would Ryoni sense the danger? Would Titus Cariad help? Would the Visitotem alert him? So many unanswered questions.

She swerved seconds from colliding with him. It seemed that she was hell-bent on making Troy fall, on shattering his resolve, on ensuring that her wicked plots remained hidden in the shadows. His own aunt, his own flesh and blood wanted to kill him.

Had she killed Jess?

The raging wind became a tormentor, trying to tear him from the back of the bird. The rain fell even harder, blinding him now with its ferocity. She had caused this. Was she the one making the ground so mushy in the Brook and so dry in Elysium Fields? The two Devout Drolles engaged in a deadly aerial dance, spiralling, circling and swooping through the sky. Troy clung desperately to his mount, his knuckles tight upon her feathers, his brow sheened with beads of sweat, his mind racing to think of something that could save him. He watched as Eliza revelled in the chaos she had unleashed. Thunder rumbled angrily. Her head was thrown back, her face alight with glee, she looked every inch the witch he knew she was.

As he gaped at the woman, the woman he thought he knew, his father's only sister, she conjured up dark tendrils of magic, using the polluted ribbons that criss-crossed the sky. She sent them snaking towards Troy's Drolle, clearly attempting to choke it, then when it was caught in the toxicity, she would use her sorcery to entangle its wings and send it plunging down to the earth. And he knew he'd crash down with it.

Thinking of his love for Blue and the desire to clear his family name, Troy fought back with all his might, summoning his own strength and calling upon the Devout Drolle's ancient connection to himself and to the planet Celestia. He prayed that The Visionary, down by the Drolle's nest could help him in some way.

"Stop this Eliza!"

Lightning sliced the sky, a white-hot bolt of power. The two birds clashed in a spectacular chaos of feathers and magic, their wings locking in a battle of wills. Their claws sharp and mean, beaks like razors. The ear-splitting calls filled the air, a cacophony of dread that made Troy shudder.

"Back off... back off and tell me where Jessie is."

Eliza's malevolent laughter polluted the air, piercing the growing darkness, as she continued to press her advantage. The stormy clouds swirled about them.

"Never."

She whispered curses and incantations, her eyes dancing upon her pale face. She was enjoying this. Her Drolle lunged forward, snapping at Troy's bird continuously with its razor-sharp beak.

Troy's heart raced as he fought to maintain control; his eyes locked upon Eliza's. He could see the depths of her cruelty, the darkness that had consumed her soul. But he refused to be swayed by her evil. He would protect his friends, save Jess, and cleanse Celestia of her damned corruption. Even if it killed him.

Would it kill him?

With a final surge of determination, Troy and his Devout Drolle broke free from Eliza's dark magic. They soared higher into the murky sky, leaving her behind, her evil laughter faded into the distance.

***

Troy's heart pounded with adrenaline as he looked down at the world below. He knew that the battle was far from over, that Eliza would stop at nothing to achieve her wicked goals.

As he continued his flight across to the other edge of the lake, he whispered a silent vow to himself and to the land he loved. He would confront the evil that threatened to consume their home, and he would do whatever it took to bring light back to their world.

No matter the cost

As Troy's feet touched the ground near Lumina Lake, his eyes scanned the area for any signs of clues or danger. The polluted waters stretched before him, a grim reminder of the toxic reality they were facing. Yet, his attention was drawn to a different sight. Here, at the other side of the huge expanse of lake, far from where they had been previously, there was a large opening in the rocks nearby. It was a large, expansive cave entrance, and there, within its depths, he spotted a group of Droids.

His heart quickened as he realised the significance of this discovery. These Droids were different from the ones used for everyday tasks in the Capital Core—the waste collectors. He believed that they were the same menacing figures that had somehow captured Jess, the ones he suspected were working under Eliza Calete's command. The pieces of the puzzle were coming together, revealing a disturbing truth that he couldn't ignore. Tears rained from the sky, a deluge of dark magic. The thuds of the fat, gloopy raindrops matched the thudding of his heart.

Troy's mind raced as he observed the Droids in the cave. What were they doing here? What was their purpose? He knew that this couldn't be a coincidence. Not after the way his aunt had tried to down him. She wanted him dead, scared of what he would uncover here.

The presence of Eliza and these eerie Droids so close to Lumina Lake, where the pollution seemed to originate, was too significant to ignore. It was as if they were guarding a secret, a secret that might hold the key to Jessie's whereabouts and the exact source of the pollution that was wreaking havoc on their land.

His instincts told him that he needed to investigate further, to venture into the cave. He turned his gaze to the Devout Drolle, a silent understanding passing between them. With a determined nod, he approached the cave's entrance, his legs trembling with a mix of anticipation and apprehension. As he ventured deeper into the shadows of the cave, the air grew markedly colder, and the atmosphere became far more ominous. The sounds of his footsteps echoed off the walls, creating an eerie symphony of rhythmic thuds.

He came to a chamber. Hiding himself behind a rock, he watched with disbelief.

The Droids were gathered in a circle, their red laser eyes casting an eerie glow in the darkness. Their movements were methodical, precise, automatic. They were focused, engaged in a specific task. They were packing something into barrels.

Other Droids stood by screens around the cavern. A huge array of screens. There he saw the faces of friends, neighbours, his workers from within the Brook. They were being watched...continuously.

Troy's heart sank as he took it in. This must be the toxic waste they were guarding, that they were hiding within these cavernous depths.

But worse than the waste, they were invading the privacy and freedoms of thousands of Celestians. Watching their every move, storing away their habits and behaviours. They were listening to their private conversations...surveilling them...ever present.

His mind flashed back to Jessie's cave drawings; her warnings etched into the rock. The rows and rows of Droids. Could this be one of the places that she had depicted? Could this be where the truth about the pollution and her mysterious disappearance lay?

As he continued to watch, he saw her: Eliza.

With his aunt now here in these caves with her Droids engrossed in those screens, plotting, Troy realised that he was safe to take to the skies once more. She surely couldn't quickly mount the Drolle before he had a chance to get back to the others.

Troy turned away from the cave entrance and headed

back outside. The icy air of the wide-open space around Lumina Lake hit his face, and he took a deep breath, trying to steady his racing thoughts. The storm had disappeared almost as quickly as it had arrived. Eliza's damn dark magic. Shards of weak sunlight now flooded the lake. He knew that he couldn't face Eliza and the Droids alone, and he needed to find a way for Titus, Blue and Ky to join him before venturing any further.

As he stood there, gazing up at the sky, he spotted the magnificent form of the Devout Drolle who had brought him to this side of the lake. It was lazily circling above, riding the thermals. Her amber and sapphire feathers caught the sunlight, creating a mesmerising dance of colours against the backdrop of the polluted sky. Troy's heart swelled with a mixture of awe and gratitude for the creature that had come to their aid.

With a sharp, piercing call, the Devout Drolle began its descent, its wings outstretched as it gracefully lowered itself to the ground. Troy watched in awe as the enormous bird touched down before him, its golden eyes fixed on him as if in understanding. The connection between them felt stronger now, a bond forged in the face of danger and adversity. The battle with his aunt had only increased his link to this creature.

Without hesitation, Troy approached the Devout Drolle, his hand outstretched once more to touch its magnificent feathers. The bird's presence was both comforting and poignant, a reminder that he wasn't alone in this fight. He could feel the energy emanating from the creature, a sense of purpose and determination that mirrored his own. How could Eliza destroy this wonderful bird's habitat?

With a deep breath, Troy climbed onto the back of the Devout Drolle, his fingers gripping the soft feathers for support. He could feel the powerful muscles beneath him, the warmth of the bird's body against his own. As he settled into place, he glanced down at Lumina Lake.

With a gentle nudge from the Devout Drolle, they began to ascend into the sky once again. The world below quickly shrank, the growing pollution of the once beautiful landscape giving way to the vast expanse of the Desire Mountains. Troy felt a mixture of exhilaration, trepidation and wariness as they soared higher, the wind rushing past him, and the world below unfolded like an ancient map. Like Jessie's map.

As they gained altitude, Troy's eyes scanned the terrain, searching for any signs of Jessie. He knew that the answers they sought might be hidden among these peaks and valleys.

As they glided through the air, Troy's mind raced with a swirl of thoughts and emotions. He thought about Jess, about the mystery she had left behind in her drawings and writings. He thought about Blue and Ky, his friends who were equally determined to find answers. And he thought about his family's dark history, the secrets that had been hidden for far too long.

With each beat of the Devout Drolle's powerful wings, Troy felt a strong sense of purpose. The bond between Celestians and the creatures of the planet was a source of strength, a reminder that they were joined to something greater than themselves.

As he continued to glide through the sky, Troy's

firm resolve grew stronger. With the Devout Drolle as his companion and guide, he knew now that they would bring justice to their land.

He was done with the dirt. Done with the dirty pasts, dirty lies and dirty secrets.

CHAPTER 31

JESS

Jess watched with a growing sense of astonishment. From her hidden vantage point, peering out of a crack in the large cavern's rough ceiling, she gaped as Troy soared triumphantly through the sky on the back of the Devout Drolle. The sight was both breathtaking and heartwarming. She couldn't believe her eyes. For a brief second, she paused, unsure. Was Troy someone she could definitely trust?

Could he be out to harm her too?

She prayed that she could still rely on her friend. She hoped that the things that she had witnessed with his company, with Eliza, didn't mean that she should be afraid of this sight of him commanding the Devout Drolle. Perhaps, what she was seeing, here and now, was Troy's determination to uncover the truth and bring an end to the darkness connected to the Calete name. But she no longer knew what was up and what was down. Confusion was now her closest friend.

Her stolen moment of awe was short-lived, as a sudden rustling behind her drew her attention back into the shadowy cavern. Before she could react, a firm hand clamped over her mouth, stifling her startled cry of surprise. Panic surged through her as she was dragged roughly backward, her captor's grip unrelenting. She struggled against the hold, her heart in her mouth as she tried to free herself. Why was this happening?

As she was forced into another hidden crevice within the rocks, her eyes widened in recognition. The woman who stood before her was none other than Eliza Calete. In the flesh. Bold as brass. Of course, It had to be. She was the lynchpin to all of this, the figure who had plotted and planned the sinister events that had unfolded in this land. The one always watching. The same woman who had taken pleasure in causing harm and chaos, all while pretending to be an employer, someone who cared for the future of Hallowed Brook.

"Well, well, Jess," Eliza sneered, her voice dripping with malicious intent. "It seems you've been quite the little meddler, haven't you? Going somewhere?"

Jess stayed silent. Her mind trying to grapple with how to respond, as she glared at Eliza, anger and fear warring within her. She had always suspected that Eliza was behind all of this, but to finally come face-to-face with her was a chilling experience. She had underestimated the extent of Eliza's malevolence, the depths to which she was willing to sink to achieve her goals. She had shown her her face this time, not hidden her identity. Surely, that wasn't a good sign. Why had she kept her alive for so long?

Eliza's grip on Jess tightened, her long, pointed nails digging viciously into her skin.

"You see, my dear, I have plans for this land, plans that don't involve the likes of you or anyone else from Hallowed Brook."

A wicked smile played on Eliza's lips as she continued, "I intend to make this land worthless, uninhabitable, desolate, dead. And once it's in ruins, the people of Hallowed Brook will have no choice but to relocate to the Capital Core."

Jess's eyes blazed with fury as she struggled against Eliza's hold.

"I've been keeping you captured in order to cause panic, worry...someone missing leads to gossip...loose talk...that's been valuable."

"No. No, you can't. You're a monster," she spat, her voice trembling with a mixture of red-hot anger and steely defiance.

Eliza's evil laughter echoed through the narrow passageway, the sound sending a shiver down Jess's spine. She was incensed.

"A monster? Oh, my dear, you have no idea. But rest assured, I have further plans for you as well. but, you've brought them here, all here, exactly where I needed them."

Then, with a cruel smile, Eliza pushed Jess backwards. The ground beneath Jess's feet suddenly shifted, and she danced in mid-air trying not to tumble. But tumble she did, she slid down the slope, down the steep descent into the darkness below.

Her screech tumbled too. Before Jess could properly react, she was thrown backward, tumbling down into the depths of the earth. Panic and dread consumed her as she fell into a maze of tunnels, her surroundings becoming a blur of shadows and darkness. She fought to regain her footing, stumbling and gasping for breath as she tried to make sense of her surroundings. Any ounce of sense at all.

She stood then looking around her. As the tunnels twisted and turned, Jess's mind raced. Eliza's plan was becoming horrifyingly clear: to create a wasteland above using the people of Hallowed Brook as worthless pawns in her twisted game. The startling realisation struck her like a physical blow, and a mixture of anger, desperation and futility made her sink to the floor. She was here again. Captured and gagged, silenced. She wanted to cry.

Instead, she moved deeper into the labyrinthine tunnels. With each step she took, Jessie's fear spiralled. At the same time, she knew that she couldn't let Eliza's plans succeed, that she had to find a way to stop her and save her friends and this land from the darkness that threatened to obliterate them. But how?

The tunnels may have been dark and treacherous, but Jess began to harden with each step. She used the shadows as motivation. The darkness as a driver. She became fuelled by a fierce determination to bring an end to Eliza's reign of terror and ensure that the light could once again shine upon this place, the home that she deeply loved.

Finally, after what felt like an eternity, her steps came to a jarring stop as she met a dead end. She hit the rocky surface before she realised. Pain radiated through her body from the sudden impact, but she desperately pushed past it, driven by her burning desire to escape.

Slowly, carefully, she picked herself up, wincing as she felt the ache in her bruised limbs.

As her eyes adjusted to the dim light filtering in from above, Jess realised that she was in a vast underground chamber. Stalactites and stalagmites jutted from the cavern floor and ceiling, casting eerie, moving shadows that danced along the walls. The air was heavy with an earthy scent, and the distant sound of dripping water echoed through the dim chamber. It took her back to those days where she wanted to end it all.

Her heart still racing, Jess took a gasping, deep breath and assessed her surroundings. She knew that Eliza must be close behind, and she needed to find a way out before her captor caught up to her. Gritting her teeth, she began to explore the cavern, her steps cautious and slow as she navigated the uneven terrain.

As she moved deeper into the chamber, Jessie's eyes caught something glinting in the faint light. She approached curiously and saw a small opening in the wall, partially obscured by a cluster of rocks. Feeling a jubilant surge of hope, she realised that it might be a passageway leading to another part of the cave system.

Gathering her courage, Jess squeezed through the narrow opening, breathing shallow breaths as she pushed herself forward. The passage was cramped and claustrophobic, and she had to contort her body to make progress. But she was driven by the knowledge that she had to keep moving, that she couldn't let herself be captured by Eliza's clutches again. She had shimmied through enough tunnels recently to know that she could do this.

After what felt like hours, but was actually mere minutes, the passage widened, and Jess found herself in another chamber. This one was larger than the last, and the walls were adorned with intricate patterns formed by natural mineral deposits. She couldn't help but marvel at the elemental beauty of this underground world, even as fear continued to gnaw at the edges of her mind, she recognised its outstanding allure. It hypnotised her.

She touched a thick, twisted jut of crystallised rock, as a chilling voice echoed through the chamber. "See. It's Impressive, isn't it?" Eliza's voice was dripping with her own self- importance, teasing her as she stepped into view, her figure illuminated by the soft glow of the ancient crystal embedded in the wall.

Jess's eyes narrowed as she faced her captor once more. This endless dance was becoming tiresome. Her voice trembling with fury and frustration she looked Eliza right in her emerald-green eyes. "You won't get away with this, Eliza. Your twisted plans just won't succeed. I know. I feel it here." She pounded upon her chest.

Eliza's laughter cut through the air, sharp and cold. The corners of her mouth twitching with mirth.

"Oh, my dear, you underestimate me. You see, I've already set my plans in motion. The toxic pollution, the destruction of the land. All of it. This has been laid out for years and years. It's all part of my sorcery. Little, brave you will never stop me. It's sweet that you think you even had a hope to."

Jess's heart sank as she realised the extent of Eliza's malevolence. Sorcery? What did she mean? Her mind grasped at threads, searching for any possible answers, desperately trying to thwart Eliza and her evil.

Then Eliza took a step closer, her eyes gleaming with wildness, glowing.

"Have you figured it out yet? What I am? What you are up against? No... shame. Not that bright, are you?"

Jess's stomach churned, bile rose, choking her. Her throat became constricted. She smelt Eliza's sour breath.

"I don't understand…"

"I didn't expect you to. The cogs are in motion and soon all will be revealed. We need a compliant population. Afraid and scared. We want them to think supplies are scarce. That they have little to look forward to. They'll believe that they don't have any options. The only option is to comply."

As Eliza rambled on, something snapped inside Jessie. Months and months of trauma and torment rose to the surface in a tempest of emotion. She couldn't allow Eliza to succeed, she wouldn't let her carry out her twisted vision. The words became a buzz of noise, her face swirling in front of Jessie's eyes. With a burst of adrenaline, a fire igniting in her belly, she lunged forward, tackling Eliza and knocking her to the ground. Jess could barely believe she'd done it.

The two women grappled in the dim light of the cavern, their movements fuelled by rage, desperation and belief in their own vision for this sacred land. Jess fought with everything she had, Eliza's sinister plans ringing like an alarm in her mind.

As the struggle continued, a loud rumbling echoed through the chamber, causing the ground to shake beneath them. Jessie's heart raced as she realised that the cave system was shifting, the natural world responding to the chaos unfolding within its very depths.

With a final surge of fierce strength, Jess managed to break free from Eliza's grip and scrambled to her feet. The ground continued to shake, and rocks tumbled from the ceiling, creating a chaotic scene around them. A catastrophe. Jess knew that she had to find a way out, she had to escape the shifting labyrinth before it became her tomb. Her muscles screamed.

With a surge of strength, she sprinted through the cavern. Weaving this way and that, she navigated the treacherous terrain with a defiant urgency. The echoes of Eliza's laughter and the sound of collapsing rocks chased her as she fought to reach the surface. To reach the light.

Finally, after tiptoeing along a precarious ledge, Jess burst into the open air, gasping for breath as she emerged from the mouth of the cave. The sunlight blinded her for a moment, but she welcomed its warmth. She looked around her, trying to get her bearings. She had escaped the depths of the earth, she had evaded Eliza's clutches, and now she knew she needed to put an end to Eliza's reign of terror.

Squinting in the morning sun, Jess turned her gaze to the horizon. The battle was far from over, and the land, their freedoms, were still at risk. But she knew that she couldn't give up, that she had to continue fighting for Hallowed Brook and for its people. And as she took her first steps forward into the light, after months in the all-consuming dark, she felt a wish engulf her. Jess would gather her strength and find her friends. Then, with their help, she would work to expose Eliza's wicked plans.

As she scrambled down towards Lumina Lake, Jess's mind raced with thoughts of Blue, Troy and Ky. She knew that Troy had flown the Drolle, she had seen him. She was sure now that earlier, she had heard Blue's voice. It was obvious, they were here looking for her. Her heart soared. She thought of the drawings, the messages she had left behind in the cave, how she had hoped that they would live on after her. But she was here, alive, fighting back, large as life.

With each step she took, Jess burned with purpose. The sight of the once-pristine landscape marred by pollution and greed only made her push onwards more quickly. She was no longer just a captive, but a brave warrior, rallying the cry for her land, rounding up those who loved it just as she did.

The Devout Drolles' calls grew louder and more insistent, as if urging her forward. It was as if the creature understood the stakes too, as if it knew the urgency. Jess couldn't help but feel a connection to the majestic bird, a connection that transcended words and crossed the boundaries between species. A connection that filled her with tenacity.

She headed onwards with a sense of wonderment., a reminder that she had the strength to make a difference, to stand up against those who sought to destroy their world.

With the sunlight in her blue eyes, Jess rounded a corner and gasped. Blue, her best friend was sitting upon a rock. But Jessie's elation turned to worry in the blink of an eye. Blue, she looked pained, more than pained, she looked in agony.

CHAPTER 32

THE VISIONARY

As Titus Cariad meditated beneath the open sky, his connection with the spirits deepened, and he was granted a sudden, clear vision, a glimpse into the depths of the unfolding turmoil. Images danced before his mind's eye, a sequence of events that were both disturbing and sinister.

In this foresight, he saw Eliza Calete, her cold eyes fixed on a struggling figure. The shadowy person was bound and helpless, lying in a shallow pit. It had to be Jess.

Eliza wielded a large shovel, layering dirt over the prone form with calculated precision. The suffocating earth covered the body, the muffled cries and desperate struggles causing Titus's heart to clench in anguish.

The earth kept piling higher and higher, and the figure's eyes, wide with terror, locked onto his gaze from within the insight. Before he could truly see, the snake hissed, blocking the face of the figure that Eliza was tormenting. The snake was Eliza, it had been Eliza all along. It was obvious now. She must have been blocking his powers with the dark powers of her own.

He sighed and cursed. The weight of the dirt pressed down, and Titus could feel the panic and despair radiating from his own core. He could feel the struggle for breath, the sense of entrapment, the agony of being buried alive. He opened his eyes.

Titus shook his meaty head, his heart thumping with the raw intensity of the vision. He understood the gravity of what he had seen. Was this the cruel plan that Eliza Calete had devised to silence Jess forever? It was a chilling revelation; a clear indication of the lengths Eliza would go to in order to protect her dark secrets.

With a desperate sense of this insight's importance, Titus knew that time was of the essence. He needed to warn Ky, Blue, and Troy; to guide them away from the path that led to Eliza and certain death... He had to share this vision, to expose the sinister plot that clearly had Jess ensnared. It was too late for Jess; of that he was fairly certain. A sadness enveloped him. Too late for her but not too late for the others. They had a chance to get away. Her evil plan was to use Jess, using her to lure them here, to lure them to this place to silence them.

Rising from his meditation, the Visionary's dedication burned brightly. He had been chosen as a conduit between the spirits and the living world, and it was his duty to ensure that justice prevailed. With a heavy heart, he set forth, he needed to find the others, give them the heart-breaking news. Ryoni pitter-pattered by his side and his staff glowed dully. Titus closed his eyes and reached down inside himself for strength. He was more tired than he had ever been, but he knew that now, more than ever, it was up to him to confront the looming darkness and protect those who were innocently staring into the face of unfathomable malice.

He had to kill Eliza. Kill her before she killed them all.

CHAPTER 33

BLUE

B lue lay on the hard, unforgiving rock, her back and neck screaming in agony. Every movement felt like a fresh dagger plunged into her spine. She had endured pain before, it had been her constant companion for many years, but this was different. It was relentless, gnawing at her like a hungry beast. She felt blinded by its piercing sharp teeth. Was this something to do with Eliza and her magic?

Troy had gone up into the skies, off on the magnificent bird, the Devout Drolle, just like she'd asked him to. He was soaring high, above the clouds, on a quest to search for answers. The giant, Titus, had left to meditate in solitude, his golden Shadow Wolf trailing at his side. Ky had taken the Lunafi to forage for food. The little creature had looked half starved, pitiful wails escaping her throat.

All of this meant that Blue was left alone, feeling utterly helpless. Her guard could be lowered, she could stop pretending for a while. She tried not to sob. Her frustration and sadness welled up inside her, a dam about to burst. If it collapsed, she knew that the opening of the floodgates could lead to her being swept away.

Sighing and counting to ten, she clenched her teeth, refusing to cry out. But the low sob told of her unbearable, needling pain. This was excruciating. She didn't want to be a burden, especially not now, not when they were so close to finding Jessie. But the tears welled up in her eyes anyway, a silent sign of her suffering. She wanted to go home. She craved the simplicity of her treehouse, the soft fur of Scruffy. As she thought about this, she was wracked by pangs of guilt. They were close... so close... so very near to finding her best friend. Jess was mere fingertips away... she imagined herself reaching out and clasping her.

As she lay there, her consciousness teetered on the edge of sleep and wakefulness. A balancing scale. Blue could barely keep her eyes open. Her body seemed to be shutting down, refusing to carry on. It was in danger of completely giving up.

It was in that twilight state that she saw Jessie, as vivid and real as life itself. As she curled in a foetal position, stifling more sobs, suddenly Jess was there.

Was her brain playing foul tricks on her? Was she dying?

She blinked and tried to sit, seeing her friend there by her side, gently stroking her back and murmuring soothing words. Encouraging her to lay down, her hushed tone was like a lullaby. For a moment, Blue couldn't believe her eyes. Was this a dream, or had she finally succumbed to the relentless pain?

Was this a vision or one of Eliza's wicked spells?

"It'll be okay, Blue," Jessie whispered, her voice like a cooling breeze on a humid, sweltering day. Her shadow fell onto the ground, as if in proof of her reality.

"You're stronger than you think Blue, you can get through this. You're an inspiration. You really are."

Blue blinked, her eyes filling with tears. "Jessie? Is this

real? Is it really you?"

But before she could receive an answer, another voice called out. A deep powerful voice as the giant's form pounded towards them. It was Titus, looking more shocked than Blue had ever seen him. His eyes were fixed on Jessie as if he had seen a ghost. His Visitotem quivered in his grip, and he looked around as if he too believed this was one of Eliza's tricks, a sorcery, a spell. Ryoni sniffed Jess and licked her sloppily on her pale, thin face.

She laughed heartily.

"Hey, quit it Mr… I know I need a bath but I'd rather it wasn't a wolf bath, cheers."

The sound was musical, tinkling, joyful. Could her ears be deceiving her too?

"Jessie? Is it really you?" Titus echoed, his voice trembling with disbelief.

Ryoni howled and licked Jess again, washing away some of the dusty grime she was coated in.

The three of them, Blue, Jessie, and Titus, stood there in a surreal moment of astonishment. It was as if the boundaries between reality and the unknown had blurred, leaving them all questioning the very nature of their world.

"It's me yes. It really is. I'm real, honest. I guess that I've got a lot to explain."

"You're not wrong there," Blue smiled as she hugged her friend tightly, inhaling her dusty scent. She wanted to hold her tight, so very tight and never, ever let go.

Blue's pain seemed to have momentarily receded, replaced by a profound sense of awe. She didn't know how or why Jessie had appeared, but in that instant, she clung to the belief that maybe, just maybe, this wasn't an illusion and Jess was actually here, plain as day, sitting in their midst. She felt real under the weight of her hug, she smelt real, she sounded real.

It seemed that they'd been closer to finding their friend than they had ever imagined.

"So, who is being buried alive by Eliza in the dirt?" Titus muttered. His moonlike face was screwed up in fearful confusion.

CHAPTER 34

TROY

Troy made his way back from the Devout Drolle's nest, his mind swirling with the newfound knowledge of the ever-watchful Droids and Eliza's ability to fly the Drolles. He considered the weight of the secrets that his Aunt Eliza was keeping within this mountain lair. He was baffled as to why.

As he walked, the air did little to clear the fog of confusion and dread that had settled over him. It buried him. Part of him felt choked, like he just wanted to come up for air, to soar, to leave this all behind.

Suddenly, from the shadows of the rocky terrain, his Aunt Eliza appeared, her presence casting a chilling shadow. Her green eyes glinted with a malevolent light, and her lips curled into a sinister smirk.

"Well, well, well, if it isn't my dear nephew again," Eliza purred, her voice dripping with intentional malice. "Right where I want you."

Troy's heart missed a beat as he stopped in his tracks, his eyes locked onto his aunt's. He couldn't shake off the feeling of unease, of the deep strangeness that seemed to radiate from her. Her aura was obsidian black.

"What do you want now, Aunt Eliza? Trying to kill me again?" Troy asked, his voice quivering with a mixture of anger, uncertainty and dread. His reedy, weak tone embarrassed him, but he swallowed it down.

Eliza Calete took an intentional step closer, her gaze never leaving his. Her green eyes boring into his hidden fears. "Oh, Troy, my boy, you still have so much to learn," she taunted. "You're a Calete, just like me. And Calete's, my dear, are magic. All of us."

Troy's eyes widened in shock. Magic? It was a word he had always associated with legends and fairy tales, not with his own family. Until recently that was. He thought that Eliza had chosen to be a sorceress, stumbled off the path, embraced darkness, but here she was saying it was in their blood. He took another step backwards, trying to get away from her toxic orbit, to make sense of her words.

"I'm Magic?" he repeated, his voice barely above a whisper. The penny had finally dropped.

Eliza's laughter cut through the mountain silence like a wicked melody.

"Yes, Troy, you are magic. The kind that runs in our bloodline, a gift passed down through the generations. You have it, just as I do."

Troy stood there, the world he had always known crumbling around him. The revelation that he possessed magic, that he was part of the same lineage as his Aunt Eliza, was like a heavy stone crushing his chest. He struggled to find his voice amidst the chaos of his thoughts.

"But... I'm not evil. No, never. And my father, Terrence... he's a good man. Where is he? Where are you keeping him?" Troy stammered, his voice trembling with a mixture of confusion and fear.

Eliza Calete merely smirked then, her green eyes

glinting with an unsettling mix of amusement and malice. She took another purposeful step closer to Troy, her presence radiating with a darkness that sent shivers down his spine.

"Oh, dear nephew, you're so naive," she purred. "You see, magic is not inherently good or evil. It's how you wield it that matters. Your father, Terrence, he knew too much, saw too much. He knew about my plans, about the pollution, my watching Droids, about everything. So, I had to deal with him. Before he had a chance to use his powers to nullify my deeds."

Troy's heart sank as the twisted pieces clattered into place. His father's sudden illness, the death of their animals, the cull, his continuing weakness, it had all been orchestrated by his aunt. Tears welled up in Troy's eyes, a mixture of grief, fury and regret.

"You... you poisoned him?" Troy whispered; his voice barely audible.

Eliza chuckled darkly. "Oh, my dear nephew, you really are slow on the uptake. I could have done but no. I didn't poison him directly. No, I simply allowed the natural pollution to take its toll. The dirt. The many, many barrels of dirt from the Capital Core. Sometimes the evil is in everyday deeds, not in magic. It was entwined into all the dirt you failed to see. The thing is, the toxins weaken the immune system, making the body vulnerable to all sorts of illnesses. Diseases. Poxes. It affects the animals and the humans who work closely with them. Such a deep shame."

Troy's fists clenched, and he took another step back, his anger flaring like a raging fire. He wanted to leave, to run.

"So, it's all you. All of it? You're responsible for all of this, aren't you? The pollution, Jessie's disappearance, everything!"

Eliza's laughter echoed through the mountain landscape, a sound that sent a chill down Troy's spine. "You catch on fast, don't you? Yes, it's all part of my grand plan. To make this land worthless, to force everyone to relocate to Capital Core, where I'll have them under my control. Longford Grimes, he will rue the day he ever trusted me. I'll set up a new business there, using the Droids and the people from Hallowed Brook to manufacture synthetic food. I'll be richer and more powerful than ever. And I'll no longer have to hide my magic away. My Droids have been gathering dirt, dirt on everyone in the Brook, further ways to persuade them to obey me. You'd be surprised at the secrets people keep Troy. I know your secret. How close you and Blue have become. It's very touching. So sweet. A shame it will all have to end though."

Troy's mind raced as he tried to process the enormity of his aunt's evil scheme. He had to stop her, for his father, for Jessie, for Blue and Ky, and for the entire realm that was at risk of being consumed by her unbridled darkness.

"You won't get away with this, Eliza," he said, his voice filled with steel. "I'll make sure of it."

But Aunt Eliza only laughed again, her laughter fading into the howling wind as she mounted another Devout Drolle, ready to continue her wicked plans.

"You have no hope against my magic, you've never even tried to harness yours. You don't stand a chance. Your sorcery is weak, partially formed, you know nothing."

He stared at her, with a mixture of shock and disbelief.

He still couldn't comprehend what she was saying. The words were like another language almost. His magic? His sorcery? Troy knew the enormity of this revelation would take a long time to fully sink in. If she let him live.

Eliza's laughter echoed out across the valley, a chilling sound that sent shivers down Troy's spine.

"Oh, Troy, you really are struggling with this, aren't you?" She smirked, her eyes glinting with a malevolent gleam. "You thought we were just ordinary folks, struggling to feed everyone, building homes, creating jobs for those living in Hallowed Brook. But the truth is, we are anything but ordinary."

She moved the huge Drolle closer, above him, towering. She peered down at him as if he were a mere worm in the dirt, her voice dripping with condescension. " This is an integral part of who we are, who the Calete family have always been. Haven't you ever wondered why we're so skilled at manipulating the land, why we've been able to profit from the disasters, the animal deaths, pollution that's been spreading across Celestia? There's power in misery. Control in people's sense of insecurity. Ways to use the knowledge of their secrets."

Troy's mind flashed back to the Brook, the polluted rivers, the toxic dirt, and the devastation that had befallen their once-pristine land. How the people here had faded, become less vibrant and free.

"You really are saying you're responsible for it all. The pollution, the suffering of our people?"

Eliza's smile widened, revealing a sinister satisfaction. "Oh, it's not just me, Troy. It's our family's legacy. We have the power to control the very elements of this world. I can communicate with the spirits of darkness, harness their energy, and use it to my advantage. Our ancestors did the same, sometimes for good, but now it's my turn to wield this power and I've chosen darkness. Niceness is so very boring, so dull. Following the rules is far too overrated."

Troy's world was crumbling around him.

"Erodan was a good man. I've heard the stories. He was a just leader. Why? Why, Aunt Eliza? Why would you use this power to harm our land and our people? Why would you do that instead of helping your community?"

From her lofty perch above him, Eliza's laughter turned mocking.

"Oh nephew, you know nothing of the true Erodan and his vision. Nothing. His desire to be adored, to rule. And why? Because, my dear nephew, there's profit to be made in chaos and desperation. The more the land suffers, the more people turn to me for solutions. They become cowed, insecure, desperate. They're willing to do anything to survive, even if it means giving up their freedoms, their rights."

Troy's fists clenched at his sides, anger and betrayal surging through him.

"You've been using our family's magic for your own gain, at the expense of our home and all of our people."

Eliza shrugged indifferently then. She didn't care.

"It's the way of the Calete family. Survival of the fittest, Troy. And now that you know the truth, you have a choice to make. Will you join me, embrace your heritage, and share in the power? Or will you stand in my way and become just another casualty of progress? Tick tock. It's decision time nephew. It was always going to come to this…always."

Troy's mind raced as he faced the impossible. The revelation of his family's sorcery had shattered his understanding of everything he thought he knew. Now, he had to find a way to confront his aunt, protect his home, and uncover the truth about Jessie's disappearance. Could he trick his aunt into believing he would stand with her? Did he have the strength within him? Could he harness the magic he possessed?

CHAPTER 35

JESS

Jessie stood there, free from the darkness that had imprisoned her, removed from the shadows, her eyes filled with the light of determination. She couldn't waste any time; they needed to stop Eliza before her sinister plans could come to full fruition. The sorceress wanted them all to be completely under her spell.

"Titus, are you here because I came to you... about my worries?" Jessie asked, her voice filled with amazement at seeing The Visionary here with Blue. "Did you come here to stop Eliza's pollution?"

Titus nodded, his aged face tense. She felt his powerful energy despite the weariness that cloaked him.

"Well, yes. It was partly to do with your visit. That and the fact that Troy came to me about Eliza. He'd found out that she was caught up in sorcery. He suspected that she was up to something, and her dark magic, her sorcery is what he discovered."

Blue chimed in then; her voice quiet as she revealed her part.

"He started to believe it was connected to you, to why you were gone Blue. We found the map, the one in the back of your scrapbook, and it led us here, here to Lumina Lake."

Jessie's face brightened, seeing the threads come

together. It was like the months of confused darkness were falling away and the dazzling light of truth was finally being revealed.

"Yes, I believe this is where the pollution became more widespread than just The Brook. I found the barrels. I knew someone in the company, someone connected to the Caletes was up to no good."

Titus looked at her earnestly then, a hint of regret tinged his words, he looked down to the floor.

"She has been blocking my visions, blocking them for a long while. When you came to me, Jess, I couldn't see anything. I thought perhaps this wasn't as bad as it actually is. I dismissed it because the spirits hadn't shown me the way. But, it was all Eliza. If only I'd realised. I'm sorry"

Ryoni howled, a bay of welcome that drew everyone's attention to the figures approaching. Jessie spotted the little Lunafi with its silvery coat, the creature scampered far ahead of Ky. A warm smile crossed Jessie's face as she reached down to pet the Lunafi's sparkling fur.

"Who is this little sweetheart? Well, it looks like a Lunafi... they can ward off evil... so I've heard anyway. They are mentioned in ancient poetry, from the time before, the days where everyone lived off the land. They're considered a sign of optimism, almost a good luck charm."

"Jess..." a shout boomed across from the shore of the lake.

Ky, racing forwards after spotting Jess, returned to the group, completely dumbstruck to see her standing there, free and unharmed. He beamed, unable to fully contain his emotions, as he pulled her into a tight, relieved hug. "Thank goodness, Jess. I swear I thought you were a goner... dead and buried. Food for the worms. I'm not gonna lie, I really did."

Jessie chuckled; her voice filled with the warmth of the hug and the joy of being free.

"Always the charmer, eh, Ky?"

Laughter rang out from all of them then, as they looked out over the milky waters of Lumina Lake. However, one question remained unanswered. Jess glanced around, her eyes searching around for Troy.

"Where's Troy?"

There was a pause. It stilled in the air like a hovering bird of prey.

"I'm worried about him, Titus admitted. Very worried. I saw something..."

But, as she listened to the giant's words, Jessie's eyes scanned the faces of her friends, she couldn't help but notice the stark signs of exhaustion and pain etched across Blue's face. Despite the joy of their reunion and the relief of her walking up to them unharmed, the physical toll of their arduous journey was becoming unmistakably evident in Blue's weary eyes. Had Eliza found some way to harm her?

"Troy," she muttered in a pained, weak voice.

In a split second, before anyone could react, Blue collapsed to the ground, her face twisted in agony. It was as if the stored-up fatigue and pain had finally caught up with her, bringing her falling to her knees. Jess tried to grab her before she hit the ground, holding her best friend upright in an awkward grip.

Panicked and desperate, Jessie turned to Titus, her voice trembling, her eyes flashing with concern.

"Titus," she pleaded, "help, can you do something? Blue's in so much pain."

Titus, rushed over his huge eyes filled with compassion, he came close to Blue's side, his worry for Troy seemed momentarily forgotten. He knelt down beside her and placed an enormous hand gently on her back, his touch caused Blue to sigh deeply.

Closing his eyes in deep concentration, Jess watched with growing fascination as he drew upon his connection with the natural world and the mystical energy that flowed through it.

The giant paused. He looked as if he was concentrating all of his power on helping Blue. The entirety of his energy was channelled towards her. A soft, soothing, glow of energy radiated from The Visionary's hands and enveloped her agonised form. The look on her face showed that the pain had begun to recede, and Jessie could see the visible relief in her friend's taut frame as the tension ebbed slowly away. It was as if the very essence of the earth was reaching out to ease Blue's suffering. The spirits of the elements pulling her to mother nature's bosom.

"Thank you, Titus," Jess whispered, her heart heaving with deep gratitude.

"Is that a little better now Blue?" Titus asked, offering her friend a reassuring smile, his bond with nature radiating in his lilac eyes, always a source of strength. "We're here for each other, Jess. We've been bonded by the search for you. Together, we'll overcome any challenges that happen to come our way. I don't know why I didn't offer her help before. But she's been so tough. So brave.

She's only now showed her true pain."

"That's my Blue," Jess laughed as she gazed with love at the face of her dearest friend.

As Blue's pain continued to lessen, Jessie turned her mind to Troy once more.

"So where exactly is Troy now?" Jess asked. "I saw him riding a Devout Drolle earlier. Then Eliza grabbed me. Should we be worried about him? What did you see Titus... you looked worried?"

Titus furrowed his brow, a blanketing shadow passing over his huge features as Jessie mentioned Troy. She watched closely as the giant took a moment to gather his thoughts before properly responding.

Titus, his lilac eyes wise, spoke with a calm and reassuring tone that belied the earlier doubt that seemed to have cloaked him.

"I did see something. But...Troy is a Calete, and he's shown great courage and resourcefulness. I believe he's capable of taking care of himself, especially when he's riding a Devout Drolle. Those creatures have an innate connection with the land, and they can protect their riders."

Blue, now looking considerably better, managed to sit up. She nodded her head in agreement, albeit with a hint of concern in her eyes.

"Titus is right, Jess. Troy's got that connection with the Devout Drolles, and he was determined to find you. We can trust that he'll do everything he can to stay safe."

Jessie couldn't help but feel a mixture of relief and unchecked worry. She knew Troy was a force to be reckoned with, but she also understood the dangers they faced, especially with Eliza's malevolent presence looming over them all like a dark cloud.

"I just hope he doesn't run into Eliza again. We need to find a way to stop her, Titus. She's been behind the pollution, the Droids, and who knows what else. We can't let her harm Celestia any further."

Titus nodded, his large frame casting a wide shadow. "Agreed, Jessie. We have to confront Eliza and put an end to her twisted schemes. But we should regroup first, gather our strength, and make a plan."

Ky, who had been quietly observing their conversation, chimed in, his shoulders tense.

"What if I head up to the nest? Try to find him. Make sure he's okay, then bring him back if he's in trouble. We can make a plan from there when we know what he's discovered."

Jessie and Titus exchanged grateful glances, appreciating Ky's readiness to take action. His eyes gazed up towards the nest site.

"Please be careful, Ky," Jessie cautioned. "I don't trust Eliza one bit, she's capable of so much evil. I believe we only know a small part of the wicked deeds she's tangled up in."

With a reassuring nod, Ky set off in the direction of the nest, the place where Troy had last been seen. Jess noticed that he had a palpable purpose in each stride. His desire to reunite their group and thwart Eliza's malevolent plans seemed to become more pressing with each upward step. Jess was impressed with his maturity, the daft, playful Ky seemed to have been replaced with a man determined to make things right. He'd changed.

Titus noticed Luna's swift departure, hurtling after Ky and the giant nodded with a knowing smile.

"She's gone with him. That's good. Luna is an intelligent creature, and she has a keen sixth sense. She'll lead Ky to safety, I'm sure they'll both be back with us soon."

Jessie couldn't help but chuckle, feeling a sense of relief.

"Yes, it seems Luna knows what she's doing. They make a good team."

Blue smiled weakly looking up at Jess. The colour was slowly returning to her cheeks.

"I hope they find him."

As they settled down, waiting, the sky over Lumina Lake began to change, the once-brown smog slowly dissipated. It was almost as if the land of Hallowed Brook itself was responding to the shift in the balance of power.

Jess breathed in the fresh air, stared up at the vastness of the sky and felt a deep sense of gratitude. She was alive.

CHAPTER 36

THE VISIONARY

"I'm going to seek more direction from the spirits," Titus murmured. He couldn't settle, he couldn't rest, he couldn't seem to focus his mind. It was like there was a magnet, pulling him towards his visions. It couldn't wait.

As Titus closed his eyes and focused on his Visitotem, a sense of serenity enveloped him. He felt the unblocked connection with the spirit world, and his consciousness began to drift beyond the physical realm. His body seemed to radiate with a soft, ethereal light.

Blue watched with rapt curiosity, despite having witnessed Titus's abilities before.

"He's communing with the spirits once more," she explained to Jessie. "He's been doing this along our journey, always trying to gain insights or guidance. He's been blocked previously. Perhaps now though it will be clear, he'll be free to see if the spirits have any wisdom to share with us."

Titus remained in this meditative state, his mind reaching out to the spiritual energies around him. He was searching for answers, seeking guidance, and hoping to unravel the tangled paths. With each passing moment, his connection with the spirit world grew stronger, and he began to receive an image, a glimpse into the events that were unfolding in The Desire Mountains.

In the midst of his spiritual communion, Titus suddenly felt a surge of distress and fear coursing through him. His eyes snapped open, and he gasped, nearly losing his balance. His Shadow Wolf paced with restless agitation, looking up towards the sky. A piercing growl reverberating in his throat.

"Troy... no..." Titus exclaimed; his voice filled with alarm. "It was Troy, always Troy."

His face turned pale, etched with panicked concern. He gulped and stood, his huge body reaching into the sky. "Where?" He murmured.

It was evident that something dire had occurred, something that demanded his immediate attention.

CHAPTER 37

BLUE

"**W**e have to go after Ky and the Lunafi now," the giant said. His eyes were filled with bleakness. "They can't find Troy on their own, we all need to go."

"What did you see?" Blue asked. Her stomach roiled and she felt an ominous sense that something was wrong. Badly wrong. She spotted that Titus gripped his Visitotem hard, almost to cover up the trembling of his hands. His huge face had turned a sickly green colour, similar to the eerie waters of Lumina Lake. He began pacing, the rumbling made the ground vibrate.

He stopped suddenly, dead still.

Blue's heart pounded as she stared at The Visionary, his usually calm demeanour now replaced with an ashen, numbness. It was like he was paralysed.

"Eliza has Troy, she has him and she's trying to kill him. "We need to move quickly," Titus said, his voice wavering, laced with a sense of urgency. " Troy is in her clutches, and her intentions are nothing short of deadly. She's using dark magic, and I fear he doesn't have long left."

"What? Eliza is going to kill Troy?"

Blue repeated the words under her breath, her voice

quivering. The absolute urgency of the situation leaving no room for doubt. She stood tall and faced the towering giant, peering up into his lilac eyes. Without wasting another moment, she urged The Visionary into action.

"Go!" Blue implored, her voice strained but sure. "Go after them. I'll only slow you down. My pain is under control for now, but if Troy's life is at stake, then I can't risk holding you back from getting to him right away. Go now."

Jess, nodded. Her eyes shining with understanding, she had quickly realised the gravity of the situation. She felt sure that Blue's pain had been made worse by their proximity to the polluted lake, or because of Eliza's dark magic.

"She's right," Jess chimed in support of Blue.

"Please Titus leave now, right away. Now!" Blue begged, her eyes filled with grave worry for Troy.

"Yes Titus. Go without us. I'll stay here with Blue and keep an eye on her. Getting to Troy as speedily as possible has to be the priority. Go!"

With a final glance at Blue and Jess, Titus called the wolf to his side, clutched his powerful staff and set off towards Ky and the Lunafi.

Blue watched them go, their forms becoming smaller and smaller as the giant's huge strides took them away from the lake.

She breathed out a deep breath. Her whole chest felt like lead, her eyes filling with tears, her throat chokingly tight. She didn't even trust herself to speak. The piling emotions threatened to completely engulf her.

To Blue, rescuing Troy from Eliza's clutches had become an urgent race against the clock.

"Please get to him..." she whispered barely audibly. "Please."

CHAPTER 38

TROY

It hadn't worked. She had seen right through him.

Troy had tried to trick Eliza, telling her that he would join her but, the very idea, that he could hope to bluff the evil sorceress that was his aunt, was frankly ridiculous. That was why he was here. Lying in the dirt, choking on dirt, being buried alive.

He thought back to his words. The words that she had seen right through. He had to face the truth, he wasn't particularly skilled at deception, not skilled at all. It didn't suit him, and his words had fallen flat sending Aunt Eliza into a frenzied, apoplectic fit of incendiary rage.

"Yes, okay, I'll join you, it's my destiny after all right?" He had muttered his eyes hard.

The Drolle under her was skittish, its wings flapping and its throat vibrating with odd vocalisations. Eliza looked unsteady upon its back, yet her eyes bored into him with a steady, unwavering intensity. She skewered him fast with her gaze.

"I mean it. Like you say, I'm a Calete. So, what else can I do? Tell me how I can serve you, show you my loyalty? I'm ready"

That had been his biggest mistake. A colossal, foolish mistake. He would blush, if he hadn't been near death, buried in toxic filth.

"Very well, I want you to use your magic. I'll show you how, exactly how. What I want, what I need, is for you to use your dark magic against Blue?" She smiled then, a smile that exposed her teeth, a row of white daggers, sharp and flashing in the light.

"How?" Troy demanded. He had tried to play along for as long as was possible. "How do I do it?"

Eliza studied him then. Her head tipped to one side as she dismounted the huge Devout Drolle. Clearly, she had a new focus. Troy tried to keep his face straight, settle his ragged breathing into a more even, rhythmic inhale and exhale. Had she looked excited for a short fleeting moment? Had she appeared partly swayed by his words?

She plucked a golden feather from the Devout Drolle's magnificent plumage. The amber glow lit up her face, making her green eyes look red for the briefest of seconds. She held out the proffered plume, a look of curiosity sheening her pale face.

"You hold this feather up to the sunlight, then you repeat an incantation. I will tell you the correct words. You will repeat them exactly, each syllable. After that, you bury the feather and Blue, well…someway or other she will come to harm."

His chest had heaved, and he'd desperately tried not to show the trembling in his fingers as he'd grasped the burnished orange feather.

"And what will happen to Blue then… what harm exactly?" He fought to keep his words even, not allow them to hitch with his overwhelming emotions.

"She'll drown. Drown in the waters of Lumina Lake. A

fitting end don't you think nephew? Buried by the waters, those tainted waters."

Troy gulped, his eyes blinking as he absorbed the words. The dreadful words. The words that she knew would make him crack.

"Tell me the spell, tell me quickly Eliza...Do it!"

His aunt beamed at him then. Something else flickered in her eyes though, something he couldn't read.

"Hmmm...now...let me think. I've changed my mind. I think instead the spell will cause you to kill her. Strangling her with your own hands then spilling her blood..."

"No!"

Eliza had cackled then, a sickening, ear-splitting cackle that almost made the rock they were standing upon shake. Her red hair blew around her, the black clothing she wore swirling and twisting as a tempest began to encircle them. The wild wind whirling, making Troy's head spin and his knees become weak. The rumbling got louder and louder and louder, the ground did indeed shake, until a pit formed behind him. The rain lashed down, hard, stabbing pellets. The pit became filled with grimy water. Aunt Eliza pushed him straight into the open earth. He fell flat on his back in the dirt.

She stood over him, spittle misting the air as she raged.

"Did you really believe that you could double-cross me nephew? That you could hoodwink me? You have no idea, no idea who or what I really am. I knew you had no intention of joining me, of coming over to the dark side. The feather was a bluff...the spell. Did you really believe it was that easy? To dabble in magic, to cast dark spells...

how could it be that easy? Tell me Troy... why does that woman have you so weak?"

He closed his eyes to her then. Closed his eyes to her caustic words, her incandescent fury, closed his eyes to her evil. The gall that rolled off her tongue tainting everything.

Instead, he pictured Blue's beautiful face, her curves, her shining hair. It wasn't him. It never would be. He may have been born a Calete and he would die a Calete, but a Calete with integrity, a principled Calete who had tried to work for good.

"What a noble man you are, noble and blinkered. A chip off the old block."

It was as if Eliza was reading his mind as she stalked around the lip of the pit, the dark pit that she had forced him into, her eyes flashing and her grip on reality seeming more and more tenuous with each second. Perhaps she had read his mind. Perhaps she could.

"Where's my father? What have you done with him?" He yelled. Maybe, if he could get her to reveal Terrence's whereabouts, there would be a hope to save him.

"Dust... dirt... dirt and dust. To what we all return. He's buried. Gone. Back to the land. All flesh returns to the dirt."

He felt his stomach sink then. Troy brought a hand up to his mouth, stifling a sob. He didn't want her to have the satisfaction of seeing his raw emotion, to see it weaken him.

"You're vile. A vile, awful woman who doesn't deserve anything. I hope whatever you are trying to achieve here is worth it. You had it all Eliza: A beautiful home in a place blessed by the bountiful gifts of Mother Nature, an idyllic life that some Celestians can merely dream of. You had the world at your feet and a future that could have been bright. All tied up, wrapped in glittery paper, handed right to you, no effort. A lottery of birth. Yet instead, you chose a path of darkness and corruption. To destroy, to maim, to kill. Let me reassure you aunt, you've chose wrong. A lonely path… the path to Sinestre."

"Quiet!" Eliza had bellowed. Troy had touched a raw nerve and Aunt Eliza had clearly had enough of his rambling attacks.

"Bury him," she ordered.

Troy looked up then and saw the Droids. The black, peg-doll Droids with the red laser slit in place of eyes. The Droids that had been gathering dirt. Toxic dirt, magic dirt and the dirt of secrets. Secrets that would give Eliza the power to manipulate everyone in Hallowed Brook.

As the black, grainy dirt rained down upon him, as the meagre light faded, as he struggled to keep his mouth closed, a thought hit him.

His only dirt was love.

CHAPTER 39

JESS

To distract Blue from her nervous fretting, Jess told her about her days in the caves. She recounted the cold, the disgusting food and the way she had talked to Blue, within her head, every single day, multiple times some days.

She told her best friend all about the matt-black droids with their eerie red lasers and why she had begun to etch her reality upon the stone. Blue listened intently, silently for the most part. Her shoulders seemed to sag slightly, and she nibbled at the skin at the edges of her fingers a little less often.

"Were you scared?" Blue muttered, almost as if they were words she was supposed to say, the polite response.

"I was terrified, utterly terrified. I could cope with the dehumanisation, the harsh weather and the sickening food, all of that was bearable. What I found the hardest, the thing that almost broke me, was the loneliness Blue. Loneliness is a killer. It's not the way we are supposed to be. Our greatest strength lies in our bonds with others."

The sky was changing again. Another fraught day slipping into the inky blackness of night. The shadows growing by the minute. Shadows around the lake and shadows in their minds. The pollution was back with a vengeance, snake-like, murky tendrils making the sky seem choked in waste.

Blue was sleepy, Jess could sense the weariness in her posture. That was good, at least it meant that she wasn't continually panicking about whether Titus and Ky would get to Troy in time. Whether they would save him.

Jessie sat there for a moment, quiet and reflective, thinking about Eliza. What had caused her to become so bitter, so obsessed with evil? She had wanted for nothing, the Caletes had a privileged life, was there something they were missing? A rational reason, an explanation. what was her motive, her goal?

"Why do you think she became this way?" Jess mused aloud.

"For some darkness there's no rhyme or reason Jess," Blue said sleepily. "Some will always baffle us with their misdeeds. Just as we have day and night, just as we have land and water...dark and light, there will always be some who embrace the other side. Revel in the opposite. There will always be those who want to walk in the shadows, the shadows hold a sense of intrigue. Like a flame's call to a moth."

***

They must have slept for a little while, nodded off as the moon rose high in the sky. Jess awoke with a start, gasping for breath like she had so many times back in the caves. She looked around her, worried that she was back there, but her eyes fell on the gently snoring Blue and she knew that that part of her life was over. One thing that her time in the dark caves had taught her was the power of friendship.

She thought about Troy then. No one had returned,

there was no news, and she was afraid to wake Blue to tell her that. Better to let her sleep in blissful ignorance, in a land where Troy was alive, unharmed and still her handsome half secret. That was another thing that Jess had realised: dreams held power, dreams could sustain you when everything else had deserted you. When the tenuous wisps of dreams were all you could clutch onto. We need dreams, without dreams we are nothing.

"Any news?" Blue asked her eyes red rimmed, her face hopeful. The shadowy spectre of pain creeping into her eyes. The healing that Titus had given her was clearly wearing off.

"No," Jess shook her head, hating to be the bearer of bad news. Her strong, resilient friend looked broken. She really did love Troy Calete.

"Hey, we can get through this, no matter what. I didn't spend three months in darkness for us to be plunged into grief now that I'm out. No way. I don't know about you but I'm starved. C'mon Blue, let's be foragers, that's what we do right? Let's see if there's any berries to eat around this lake. When the guys get back, they're going to need some sustenance."

Blue nodded and she stood stretching the kinks out of her back and neck. Jess could see that she was masking the pain again, putting on a brave face.

The cold of the night chilled Jess, but she was used to it now, she had become acclimatised to life in The Desire Mountains. She relaxed her shoulders and led her friend across to some Mannaberry bushes. The orange, sweet berries would give them some much-needed nourishment.

"Jess…" Blue said in an eerie voice. "Jess why is that

thing staring at us?"

Jess dropped the succulent berries, and a shrill shriek escaped her lips.

A Droid was sitting bold as brass in the centre of the bushes. Watching.

CHAPTER 40

THE VISIONARY

Titus Cariad had caught up with Ky and the Lunafi very quickly. In rapid, clipped sentences he had explained Troy's predicament and told Ky exactly where he thought Troy was being buried.

"It's in a chamber, below a rocky outcrop where one of the Drolles has their nest. I saw it clear in my vision. Vividly clear. Nothing was blocking the detail this time; nothing barred my true insight."

"So where do we go?" Ky asked looking around him, ready to go wherever Titus directed him. The Lunafi twisted around his ankles, rubbing her face against his legs, making low meeping noises.

"It's just across that ridge, across the ridge and behind that large rock stack. That's where the other nest lies."

They carried on determinedly, Ky grasped the little Lunafi in his strong arms to speed up their trek, Titus led the way. As he pounded the gravelly ground, the giant thought about all the things that might await them over on the other side. He hoped they could save Troy and that he had a chance to end the evil that Eliza had wrought across Celestia.

They heard her before they could see her. Titus recognised the sorceress's cackle; it sounded like breaking glass. Ryoni crouched low, his hackles raised and his snout pointing forward. The Shadow Wolf wanted to race towards Eliza, to pounce, Titus called him back with a soft, gentle whistle. The golden beast stopped; his eyes downcast.

"Heel Ryoni, heel," Titus said. The giant was afraid that if Ryoni raced at her, knocking her into the pit, they may not get the chance to save Troy. Her magic was unpredictable. His head swirled, he wanted to proceed with caution.

The Visionary, knew that time was of the essence as he followed the guidance of his visions from the spirit realm. The urgency in his heart matched the frantic pace of his steps, each one carrying him closer to where Troy's life now hung in the balance. Ky struggled to keep up with the giant's mighty strides. Titus turned to see him sprinting, sweat upon his brow.

As Titus finally approached the scene, by the Devout Drolles' nest, he was faced with something he hadn't seen in his visions. Mechanical Droids, matt-black waste collectors from the Capital Core, surrounded Troy, their cold, metallic limbs working tirelessly to cover him with choking, toxic dirt. His face was barely visible and what could be seen was waxy and pale. He was barely breathing.

Eliza Calete stood nearby, her dark sorcery guiding the relentless Droids in their gruesome task. Her red hair was wild, her green eyes flashing with venom. She was so engrossed in overseeing the death of her nephew, that, at first, she failed to spot the giant's approach.

"You!" She seethed as Titus appeared on the rocky ridge. "I might have known that the great Titus Cariad would try to stop me. Seems I'm just going to have to give you a taste of demonic forces for a change."

Before she had chance to act, without the slightest flicker of hesitation, Titus unleashed a magic stream from his Visitotem, attempting to disrupt the malevolent force controlling the Droids. But the technology that powered them was unnatural, making them too formidable. Their robotic actions were synchronised with a man-made precision that made them immune to his efforts. He needed help, and he needed it fast. These Droids were not of Celestia, they were constructed, designed, impossible to overpower.

Titus froze for a second, hesitating. His huge brain became blank, as if all of his years of knowledge had been sucked out through his nostrils. He trembled... floundering.

In a stroke of luck, Ryoni, the trusty Shadow Wolf, sprang into action after sensing his master's incapacitation.

With a strident series of sharp, barking commands, Ryoni rounded up the mechanical Droids, confusing their programming, the matt-black robots complied. Ryoni continued to draw them away from Troy. The Visionary looked on, pride swelling in his chest despite his sense of stalled confusion. It was almost as if he were a machine, a machine that had suffered a catastrophic failure. Ryoni's courageous actions were a reminder of the powerful bond between The Visionary and Shadow Wolf, a strong, unrelenting bond that transcended the boundaries of man-made technology.

With the Droids momentarily distracted, his mind

seeming to spring back into life, Titus seized the opportunity to strike. He directed all of his mystical energy into a single, focused burst of magic, targeting the dark sorcery that held Troy captive. The force of his will shattered Eliza's control, freeing Troy from the clutches of certain death. The dirt fell away, allowing him to stand.

Gasping for breath and covered in dirt, Troy was pulled up by Ky, his friend grasping hold of him tightly and hauling him out of the pit, to safety.

"That was a close one buddy," Ky smiled, patting the coughing Troy upon his back.

"Eliza...my aunt...stop her," Troy spluttered. Titus gaped as Eliza threw herself onto the back of her Devout Drolle. With her evil laugh ringing out across the whole valley, she grasped the bird's nape, urging it to fly.

But, she had not noticed Luna, the silver and purple furred Lunafi. She had not realised that the Lunafi had also climbed up onto the Drolle and was attacking Eliza with a whirling fury. Biting, scratching, lunging, tearing, clawing, Titus watched as little Luna launched a full scale attack. The creature tugged at Eliza's red hair, clawed at her green eyes, left huge welts and bite marks across her pale skin. The Drolle took to the sky as Eliza screamed and roared, her grip on the bird was weak and after minutes of relentless, ruthless mauling by the lithe little Luna, she tumbled to the ground with a bone-jarring thud.

Eliza held her hands up to her face desperately trying to stop the attack of the previously timid animal. Titus could hardly believe his eyes. The Lunafi was, without doubt, a curious creature.

Using his Visitotem, he sent a surge of divine energy

in the direction of Eliza. A temporary holding spell would keep her in the bubble, a mystical force field, for at least an hour. Enough time for Titus to take her down to his hut before figuring out what he should do with her.

With the threat of Eliza Calete temporarily neutralised and the Droids under Ryoni's watchful eye, Titus gestured for them to make a hasty retreat from the rocky ledge. Titus stopped, slinging their tormentor over his broad shoulders. The bubble of magic making it easy. Luna, the brave Lunafi, had managed to escape unharmed, and she danced in circles around Troy's mucky legs, trilling and meeping.

"Good Luna," Troy breathed. "Brave Luna."

Titus left the stalled Droids, called his Shadow Wolf, and indicated that they should leave.

"Back to the lake, then back to the Brook."

Back on the shores of the milky Lumina Lake, Jessie and Blue had their own surprise waiting.

Titus saw their eyes widen at the captured Eliza Calete, their glances nervously looking for reassurance that she couldn't harm them.

"She's contained, for now."

Titus Cariad's ancient heart was warmed by the way Blue raced to the grimy Troy, grasping him by the shoulders as she pulled him into a loving embrace.

"I was so worried Troy, so, so worried," she whispered, her lips grazing his neck. He saw love in her eyes.

"So, we kind of have a Droid," Jessie said with a sheepish look on her face. It was clear that she wasn't sure if they had been meant to capture the matt-black machine that had been hiding in the bushes.

"These things are recording us, taking images, listening... creepy, damned things."

The sinister Droid that they had captured looked rather pitiful. These man-made Droids that had played a role in Eliza's malevolent plans were mere useful machines, following orders. But, along with Eliza herself, it was a vital piece of evidence, a symbol of the dangers they had faced and the mysteries they had yet to unravel. It would help bring Eliza to justice.

"Longford Grimes needs to know all about what has happened here," Titus announced. "The Capital Core was in danger from Eliza's treacherous plans too."

"Can you send a messenger bird to the Capital Core? Ask Longford Grimes to meet us in the gathering place in Hallowed Brook. He can decide what to do about Eliza and the threat these Droid's pose."

"Great plan Troy, quite the leader when you put your mind to it aren't you young man?" Titus smiled.

"It seems so, and well...it also seems that I'm magic too...who knew?

"Well of course I did," Titus grinned. "It's part of your heritage. But, that's a tale for another day. Let's get down from these damned mountains. I've had quite enough of this cold air. More than I can stomach. And... I don't know about you, but I'm half-starved."

CHAPTER 41

BLUE

B lue didn't know if it was day or night. She didn't know what the next few weeks had in store for her and her friends. She didn't even know if she had a job to return to in the Elysium Fields...hell she didn't even know what was up and what was down right now. But, she knew one thing for certain. The two people that she loved most in the world were back by her side. No matter what the future held, that was a stroke of magic.

Magic... she mused. Did she hear Troy say that he was magic?

She held tight to his rough, brown hand, stole glances at his chestnut eyes, walked alongside him with a spring in her step and a sense of growth. Sometimes, when you think you've been buried, you've actually been planted. That's what Blue held onto now. The very thought swirling around her exhausted mind made her feel lighter. She had emerged from the dirt stronger; she had emerged with her head held high, and she had emerged with her blue eyes absolutely driven to keep basking in the light.

***

Longford Grimes had come from the capital causing no end of excitement in Hallowed Brook.

Longford Grimes, Celestia's President who resided in

The Capital Core was a man of imposing presence. Blue had watched him closely. His tall and broad-shouldered frame commanded attention wherever he went. He carried himself with an air of authority, as if the world revolved around his every word and action.

She spotted that he was a vain man. His once jet-black hair had long since turned a distinguished shade of silver-grey, giving him an aura of wisdom and experience with a steely hardness laced into his half smile. A smile that didn't fully meet his eyes. His hair was neatly combed back, revealing a high forehead that accentuated his sharp, intelligent features. His piercing grey eyes were like polished titanium, capable of cutting through the thickest veils of deception.

She wasn't sure she trusted him.

Longford's chiselled jawline bore the faint lines of age, but his complexion remained remarkably smooth, a sign of his life of privilege and comfort in the Capital Core. His thin lips often curved into a sly smile, revealing a glimmer of the shrewdness that lay beneath his charismatic facade. Blue stored all these details away like a secret seed.

He had arrived dressed in an impeccably tailored suit, exuding a non-nonsense air of power and sophistication. Blue listened intently as he spoke to them all. Longford Grimes was a man who knew how to make an impression, and he did so effortlessly, leaving an indelible mark on the gathered group as they retold their tale.

Titus clasped his hand tightly as he left kneeling down to his level, grateful that he had come with such urgency.

Blue watched as Eliza was led away spitting and hissing, her hands tied behind her back, just like Jess had been tied for those long months in the caves. She hoped Eliza would realise the poetic justice as she sat in her cell in the Capital Core, she hoped she never again saw the light of day.

There were still so many things to discuss, so much to deal with, healing from what had happened here would take time. For now, they all huddled on a bench, in Hallowed Brook, watching Longford Grimes give orders to a group of Capital Core guardians.

They sat there for a long time, until the crowd around them thinned, until the dipping sun shifted and the light changed. Until they finally felt their eyes could meet again, without the sheen of tears.

Blue lost track of time after a while, happy to be home, mourning for all that they had lost, grateful for the things that they had gained and thinking about what tomorrow may bring. In each of her hands, left and right, she clasped the palms of the people who made the murky parts of life still worth living.

The people who made this rise from the dirt worthwhile.

CHAPTER 42

AFTERWARDS

"How could you be so damned careless?" Longford Grimes spat. Each word was like a lash. "All these years of planning and you go and ruin things in the space of a few days."

He paced the Capital Core prison corridor, directing his words at a figure behind the enchanted bars. His grey eyes flashed menacingly, his fury building with every stride. A blob of spittle sat upon his lips. It mesmerised her.

"No," Eliza Calete said firmly, refusing to be cowed by this pathetic man. "No, you messed up Longford, not me."

He looked then like he might explode. His silver-grey hair flew from its pristine hold, as he turned on his heel and placed his face close to the magical bars. The blob of spit had disappeared, vanished, leaving only his thin, dry lips.

"You got sloppy. You got arrogant. You captured the damned girl. That's why all of this went so catastrophically wrong. That's on you Eliza."

She stood then, meeting his gaze.

"You were the one who insisted I pick up those barrels. You were the one who practically begged me to collect that shipment of toxic waste at short notice. So, I used Jess."

"You underestimated her. You didn't consider that she'd go digging."

The silence stalled in the air. A heavy silence laced with many things unsaid. The truth was they'd both made mistakes, both got greedy and overconfident. They'd both ached for control.

"I guess the question is now, how do we get things back on track?" Eliza said slyly, her emerald eyes gleaming. "How do we wrestle this around so that we can plough onwards? Get them here, control the food. Sell off the land."

He stamped his foot then, stamped his foot and clutched at his hair is exasperation.

"You just don't get it do you Eliza? They're asking questions… delving into the past, into all the secrets, the lies, gathering dirt."

"And?" She smirked.

"And… they're figuring out that people have died because of this, parents, grandparents…their flesh and blood. They're questioning the shut downs and the requirement to only eat vegetables, insects and worms. They're onto us Eliza."

She watched him, he was unravelling, unspooling, becoming uprooted. Perhaps she could use this to her advantage.

"Where's the golden sundial?"

Longford stopped then. He peered at her like she was a small, insignificant bug under his shoe.

"What sundial?"

She grinned.

"The one that's been used for years to affect

Hallowed Brook and the mountainous region above. My family's sundial, gifted years ago to Titus Cariad. A conduit of Calete magic through which we can channel our desires and direct The Visionary and the people of Hallowed Brook to follow our will. The only reason this all fell apart was because the golden sundial was moved. Find the sundial, return it to its rightful spot and we are back in the game."

"The golden sundial..."

"Correct!"

ABOUT THE AUTHOR

Michelle Haskew

Michelle Haskew is an educator, an avid reader and has adored creative writing since being very small.

Fulfilling her dream of moving to live by the sea, she spends most days upon the beautiful beaches of the Isle of Anglsey. Inspired by the possible destruction of Penrhos Coastal Park and the habitat of precious creatures, Michelle set about writing a fantasy adventure novel that deals with issues of habitat loss, corporate greed and pollution.

Printed in Great Britain
by Amazon

27836744R00149